Other *Leisure* books by Mike Kearby:

RIDE THE DESPERATE TRAIL
THE ROAD TO A HANGING

Ambush at Mustang Canyon

MIKE KEARBY

LEISURE BOOKS NEW YORK CITY

For Joe, who makes my heart soar.

A LEISURE BOOK®

January 2009

Published by

Dorchester Publishing Co., Inc.
200 Madison Avenue
New York, NY 10016

ISBN 10: 0-8439-6184-8
ISBN 13: 978-0-8439-6184-3

Printed in the United States of America.

10 9 8 7 6 5 4 3 2 1

Visit us on the web at www.dorchesterpub.com.

ACKNOWLEDGMENTS

The only people with whom you should try to get even are those who have helped you.
—John E. Southard

Many thanks to:
Mindy Reed, Fred Tarpley, Weldon L. Edwards,
and Stephanie Barko.

Ambush at Mustang Canyon

The buffalo are disappearing rapidly, but not faster than I desire. I regard the destruction of such game as Indians subsist upon as facilitating the policy of the government, of destroying their hunting habits, coercing them on reservations, and compelling them to begin to adopt the habits of civilization.

—Columbus Delano, Secretary of the Interior, Speaking before Congress in 1874

Prologue

Near Flint Creek, Texas, January 1871

The Owl Prophet, Maman-ti and twenty-five Kiowa warriors crept from the morning shadow of the scalped mountain and into the dry grasses of the Comancheria. A generous north wind concealed the raiding party in a rolling wave of yellow and allowed them to move undetected through the prairie.

Maman-ti the hero at the Battle of the Washita had saved many women and children in Black Kettle's camp from the brutal fury of Custer's Seventh Cavalry. After that day, he assumed the power of shaman and organized many raids against the *Tehá-nego*. The Owl Prophet's medicine was strong and he could predict the victor of a battle and the number of casualties on each side.

Now his visions foretold of the freighters who would camp near the scalped mountain this morning and of a wallow that would protect the Kiowa from the death spirit.

Forty yards from their intended targets, a narrow draw ran parallel to the soldiers' road. The draw was protected on the south by a stand of scrub oak. He signaled to the twenty-five with a clenched fist, and one by one the Kiowa braves crawled into the trench.

Above them, three *Tehá-nego* sat around a small fire and drank black water as they disturbed the prairie with loud laughter. An unhitched wagon loaded with goods sat behind the men. Four staked horses grazed nearby.

Maman-ti studied each man's face and recognized the one known to the Kiowa as Britt Johnson. He smiled broadly, for the Kiowa held a bounty on this *Tehá-nego* scalp. Two nights earlier, a dream vision had predicted Johnson's fate.

Maman-ti bared his teeth and shot an anxious glance at the braves on either side of him. He raised his right hand, now painted white and cloaked in the dried skin of an owl. The warriors eagerly nodded their confidence at the strongest of Kiowa signs, the owl puppet.

"*Àho!*" the Owl Prophet whispered.

"*Àho!*" replied the twenty-five.

The owl puppet motioned to the east, the south, and the west, then each line of warriors slithered to their assigned compass points.

Maman-ti raised his head and looked to the sky for a sign. On the eastern horizon, a large cloud sat on the mountaintop.

It is a good day, he thought and then signaled the attack. Soon, the *Tehá-nego* would expend their bullets, and the Kiowa warriors would fulfill the prophecy. *After this day, the whites will fear the Owl Prophet's medicine for many years, and the name Maman-ti will make even the strongest of men tremble.*

Chapter One

Elk Creek, Indian Territory, June 1874

A deafening roar rose from the canyon floor near Elk Creek as an unstoppable wall of buffalo thundered west across Indian Territory. The great beasts dispatched a mile-long swirl of dust skyward as they stampeded toward the North Fork of the Red River.

Maman-ti, accompanied by Kiowa war chiefs, Big Bow and White Horse, sat atop their ponies on the canyon rim and watched five Comanche warriors pursue the great herd.

Maman-ti, in contrast to the tall, muscular Kiowa on either side of him, stood only five-foot, seven-inches and was slender in build. His small, bronze face carried the wrinkles of many suns and made him appear much older than his age. His cheekbones protruded forward in small circles and a coarse head of black hair flowed down his back. Two owls adorned his bare chest, painted with a mixture of animal grease and crushed berries.

At the back of the stampede, hidden in the dust, the lead Comanche rider encouraged his pony close to a group of young bulls. The warrior raced into the pack and in a deft maneuver positioned his pony between one bull and the panicked herd.

The startled young bull ducked left in a splay

of dirt and on impulse slashed his horns at his pursuer. The veteran warrior anticipated the buffalo's tactic and quickly reined his pony, slowing to a position slightly behind the young bull and isolating it from the main herd.

Enraged and desperate, the bull dug his hind legs into the soft earth and in a nimble movement spun about to face his tormentor. He pawed furiously at the ground and kicked great billows of dirt onto his back as a warning.

The remaining Comanche riders raced up and surrounded the buffalo. Encircled, the angry young bull bellowed, snorted great puffs of steam from his lungs and swung his head menacingly from side to side.

The lead Comanche warrior removed an arrow from his quiver and raised it high above his head. He fitted the arrow in his bowstring and began a slow rhythmic chant.

> Come, come, come, my brother.
> Come and hear my song.
> Come running down the prairie
> And let me honor you.

The buffalo instinctively turned in a tight circle, snorting and watching each predator's movement. When the animal turned away, the lead warrior shot a flint-tipped arrow into the beast's back just below the shoulder.

Shocked, the animal jumped and issued a deep guttural howl then lowered his head and charged his attacker.

The warrior re-fitted an arrow and raced toward

the maddened bull. He passed the animal on the left and sent a well-placed shot behind the beast's shoulder and down into its heart. The buffalo stumbled, tried to regain its feet and bellowed once more.

"A bad sign?" Big Bow asked, staring transfixed at the spectacle below.

Maman-ti nodded. "I thought Big Bow doubted medicine signs."

"Big Bow may say he rejects Maman-ti's prophecy, but inside he knows the Owl Prophet carries strong medicine." White Horse slapped his chest and smiled at Big Bow. "The many Kiowa victories over the whites speak loudly to this."

Big Bow shifted uncomfortably on his mustang at White Horse's pronouncement of Maman-ti's magical power. The Kiowa war chief had fought in many battles and his muscular body showed many scars. He shook his lance toward the canyon floor and glared at White Horse. "Only a Kiowa's courage wins victories, not a dead owl."

Maman-ti smiled and glanced up at the cloudless sky. "It is too early for the sun dance. The Comanche make a sham of our custom." He swept an upward palm toward the Comanche warriors. "Their medicine will be weak because they do not give proper honor to the spirits."

On the canyon floor, the buffalo killer stood over the dead beast and withdrew a large knife from his belt. He made a slash across the bridge of the animal's nose, then ran the blade all the way to the animal's tail. When he had scalped the young bull, he rolled the hide into a bundle, held it high over his head and re-mounted his pony.

With the sun at his back, the buffalo killer rode to the east and the intertribal camps.

The remaining four warriors followed at a respectable distance behind the buffalo killer. They chanted of their victory in a high-pitched song.

> Thank you Great Spirit
> for the medicine gift
> from my buffalo brother.
> I honor him with this song.

"The Comanche should have listened to the Owl Prophet." Maman-ti shook his head in disbelief. "The ceremonial buffalo must be killed with one shot."

"So what does your owl tell you?" Big Bow asked in disdain.

Maman-ti kept his focus on the canyon floor and ignored Big Bow's disrespect. "The wolf prophet of the Comanche, Esatai, will be turned away by the buffalo spirit; the Comanche will suffer greatly for their disobedience. Quanah is blinded by revenge and uses the sun dance for war, not prayer. Any who follow him to the Adobe Walls will suffer as well."

White Horse had aligned with the Comanche years earlier, but still loathed their arrogance. Now he grinned, satisfied with Maman-ti's prediction. "What would the owl puppet have the Kiowa do?"

Maman-ti looked to the east. "We will stay on Elk Creek and hold our sun dance at mid-summer as our tradition demands."

"We should be fighting the whites, not dancing."

Big Bow snarled. "Each day more white hunters come to our land and kill our buffalo."

"Patience, Big Bow. The owl puppet will speak again after the sun dance. And he will show Maman-ti the place of the next Kiowa victory."

Chapter Two

Near the convergence of Wolf Creek and the Beaver River, Camp Supply rose majestically from the western prairie of the Cherokee Outlet. The imposing fortification featured a palisade of vertical timbers that surrounded the camp headquarters and parade ground. The stockade towered ten feet into the air and the adjoining blockhouses each held a four-foot parapet.

From a ridge south of the camp, Free Anderson, a mustanger, whistled loudly at first sight of the military stronghold. Even in the rising morning heat, the camp seethed in a blur of activity.

"That," he said to partner and friend, Parks Scott, "is a might more than a camp."

"You think the army is trying to keep the Indians out or the soldiers in?" Parks stared at the sprawling complex of tents, blockhouses, storehouses and soldiers quarters.

Free laughed. "Whichever it is, I bet they do it with little fuss."

The men had left their homes in West Texas four days earlier and ridden three hundred miles to the United States Army's "Camp of Supply." Parks led a string of seven mustangs for delivery to the army's chief civilian scout, Amos Chapman.

Free and Parks' mustang business, S&A Mustang Works, had prospered as the army continued to increase its presence over the Western frontier. Their company operated out of Free's homestead on the old Comanche Reservation in Throckmorton County, Texas.

Parks was a natural mustanger and developed his own method of capturing the wild beasts. "Walked down" was how he described the process. During the heat of summer, Parks would post a rider at a mustang watering hole. The horse's fear of man kept them from going to the water, and the animals would circle for days, waiting for the human to leave. Once the rider departed, the thirsty horses would rush forward and drink their fill. After days without water, the cool liquid expanded in a mustang's belly. Parks then roped these lethargic horses without subjecting them to a stressful chase.

These brutish horses, called the "nomads of the plains," could run a hundred miles a day over the harshest terrain and never show the worst for it. An S&A mustang was the ultimate prairie mount and the only horse that could run an Indian pony down over any distance. Since 1871, the S&A mustang had become the horse of choice for civilian and Indian scouts on the Southern plains.

Free and Parks met Chapman in the fall of 1873 at Fort Griffin where Parks had held an exhibition for the 10th Cavalry. After demonstrations of cutting and racing, Horse, Park's personal pony, drove a group of Longhorns from one end of the parade ground to the other without a rider and then herded them into a makeshift corral. When one steer tried to exit the rope pen, Horse grabbed the steer's tail and dragged the animal back into the enclosure.

The S&A mustangs had so impressed Chapman that he sought out both men after the show and promised an order from Camp Supply when he returned to Indian Territory. Free still remembered the scout's words, *"A man scouting alone on the Cherokee Outlet and the Panhandle Plains of Texas needs a pony that can get from one end of the prairie to the other in quick order."*

Free and Parks clucked at their ponies and rode down from the ridge. They approached the southwest corner of Camp Supply and crossed the Fort Dodge supply trail. A long row of canvas tents rippled in the hot June wind on the far side of the military road. To the west, the lodge poles of a tipi towered above the tents and rose in stark contrast to the military structures.

Free pointed at the tipi and grinned. "I think we've found Amos's quarters."

The men dismounted and walked their ponies through tent row, past the bivouac where several columns of soldiers drilled on the trampled prairie. In the distance, a thin figure dressed in beaded buckskin brushed a tall-speckled mule.

"Amos!" Free called.

Amos Chapman, army scout and interpreter, was of mixed blood and married to the daughter of Cheyenne chief, Stone Calf. Amos was a valuable asset to the military. His knowledge of the two cultures helped bridge the gap of understanding between field commanders and their superiors. Around Camp Supply, Indians and soldiers alike called him "Squaw Man."

Chapman turned and grinned. "Free. Parks," he said. He bowed at the waist and gave a long sweeping gesture of his arm. "Welcome to Camp Supply."

"How are you?" Free dismounted and walked up to the buckskin-clad scout.

"I can still air my lungs and I retain a fine head of hair." Amos extended a hand in Free's direction.

"That is a fine accomplishment in this country." Free shook the army scout's hand.

"And those must be my mustangs." Amos looked past Free at the string of ponies.

"The best of the best." Parks hopped off Horse and offered the string to Amos.

The scout carefully eyed the stock. "These mustangs have traveled from Texas in hundred degree heat and they still look as fresh as a daisy, Parks," he said. "Better than the Cayuse the army provides for me."

"Take the grulla for your own, Amos. She's the top of the lot." Parks untied a series of half hitches holding the ponies on the string.

Amos accepted the woolly gray mare and brushed his hand along her short back. "She's ugly as a mud fence," he chuckled.

"Don't judge her by looks, Amos. This girl will outrun any horse on the Cherokee Outlet."

"You made a believer of me last fall at Fort Griffin, Parks. I'd be proud to sit atop her."

After the mustangs were distributed to Amos' scouts, the men stood in Indian fashion around a Cheyenne cooking pot and speared large cubes of meat with their knives. "Seems a man would fare well defending himself here," Free said.

"The Indians know that as well." Chapman pointed around the camp. "In the mornings, the Cheyenne and Kiowa come in peaceful like and trade with the merchants. In the afternoon, they ride the supply trails, stealing horses and other goods. The next day, they're back in camp ready to trade again."

"That has to be aggravating to a soldier," Parks said.

"It's just the Indian way," Amos replied. "They don't regard stealing in the same light as you or I. To them, a man who can't defend his own belongings does not deserve to own them. That noise you hear echoing across the prairie is the sound of two cultures butting heads like a pair of rutting bulls. It's a . . ."

"Scout Chapman!" A deep voice boomed from tent row.

The men's attention turned to the interruption and watched as a tall lieutenant with a bushy mustache strode toward them.

"Lieutenant Baldwin," Amos greeted him respectfully.

The lieutenant walked past Free and Parks, oblivious to the two, and approached Amos. "May I have a word?"

"Certainly, Lieutenant. But, first please meet the mustangers I told you about."

The lieutenant turned and looked at the two Texans. "Oh. Yes, please excuse my rudeness, gentlemen." The lieutenant touched the brim of his hat. "It is my pleasure." He feigned a smile.

"Amos has spoken very highly of you and your mounts."

"Thank you, Lieutenant," Free responded. "Please don't let us interrupt your business."

The lieutenant nodded politely and then turned his attention back to Amos. "I need to ask that you make preparations at once to ride out to Adobe Walls."

"What's the difficulty, Lieutenant?"

"According to Bill Lee, two Cheyenne braves were in his store this morning. They were going on about a war council on the Elk Creek and how the Comanche were going to hold a sun dance."

"What? The Comanche have never held to the sun dance tradition, sir."

Lieutenant Baldwin stared into the scout's eyes. "There's something going on that I don't quite understand, Amos. Nevertheless, we have between twenty and thirty civilians in Adobe Walls, three hundred or more Cheyenne missing from the reservation and a council of Southern tribes at Elk Creek. Something has the Indians riled and we need to warn the folks at the trading post."

"I understand, sir." Amos stared at the ground. "My good friend Billy Dixon is at the Walls. I'll make ready to leave right away."

"Thanks, Amos. Bill Lee said you'd be the one to send."

"What?" Amos jerked his head up, wanting to make sure he understood the lieutenant correctly.

"Bill Lee said you'd be the man to go down to warn Billy and the others."

Amos squinted and held his thoughts for a few

seconds. "Did Bill offer when this attack would happen?"

"He indicated that the braves bragged about many buffalo hunters dying after the new moon."

"I see." Amos drew a deep breath and bit down on his bottom lip.

"I'll send a detail of four men with you."

"I appreciate that, Lieutenant. Tell them we'll leave as soon as they can get their gear ready."

"And, Amos, after you warn the civilians, I need you back here post haste." The lieutenant whirled and nodded to Free and Parks as he walked back toward the camp. "Gentlemen," he offered.

Parks watched the lieutenant disappear into the field of tents and then said, "The new moon is only two days away, Amos."

"That's a fact, Parks." Amos' forehead wrinkled as he stared at the departing lieutenant.

"What's got your back up, Amos?" Free asked.

"Something smells like skunk eggs, Free. Why would the Cheyenne tip off the military to the sun dance and an attack on Adobe Walls?"

"What do you mean?"

"Why does Bill Lee want me sent to the Walls?" Amos snapped out of his contemplation and looked at Free and Parks. "I don't trust Bill Lee any farther than I can see him."

"What's his gain from this?" Free asked.

"That's his competition selling in the Walls. And Billy Dixon and I are the ones who led those people down out of Kansas to set up their establishments."

Parks rubbed his chin trying to make sense of Amos' words. "Are you saying that Lee . . . ?"

"I'm only saying," Amos interrupted, "that Bill Lee has a lot to profit if the Indians send a raiding party to Adobe Walls."

Free looked over at Parks and then back to Chapman, "You're going to need more than an escort of four soldiers if the lieutenant is right."

Parks stepped up and stood shoulder to shoulder with the scout, "You might need some Texas help in protecting that fine head of hair."

Free slapped a hand on the scout's back and gazed at the grulla pony feasting on prairie grass shoots. "It's foolish for a man to ride headlong into trouble without friends beside him."

Amos laughed. "Better'n watching a mule's tail all day, Free."

Free grinned, walked over to the grulla and grabbed the pony's rein. "I guess it does at that." He led the mustang over to the tipi where a cavalry saddle and blanket lay on the ground. "We're heading back to Texas anyhow; I figure it might do us both good to see fresh scenery on the return." He tossed the saddle on the pony's back. "If nothing else, we'll make for good conversation down the trail."

"A man on the prairie never turns away company, Free. But you've got a wife and son waiting for you back home in Texas . . ."

"And a friend that needs help here." Free tightened the cinch strap around the pony's girth and then looked over the saddle at Amos. "So, are you too headstrong to ride without us?"

This isn't your scrap," Amos stated sternly. "I can't ask that you and Parks risk your necks for nothing.

"It's not for nothing, Amos." Free straightened and placed the bit in the grulla's mouth. "I aim to watch over my horse until the army pays for her."

Amos grinned. "Appears you know the government better than most, Free."

Chapter Three

The Old City, Texas, June 1874

A fiery mid-afternoon sun blared down and re-cast the greening Texas landscape to a palette of yellow and brown. The intrusive rays crept beneath the brim of Free's hat and robbed him of water and energy. An unceasing, glistening stream of sweat ran from his forehead, down his nose and onto his buckskin shirt. He dragged a shirtsleeve over his face in a vain attempt to stem the continual flow and keep his eyes free of the stinging salt. The messenger detail had left Camp Supply at noon and followed the winding banks of Wolf Creek downstream into the Panhandle Plains and toward Adobe Walls.

At the last high bend before the creek played out, the detail rode through a valley of grass mounds that marked the ruins of a long abandoned city. Rock slab structures jutted from the landscape and littered the prairie for hundreds of yards.

"This is our marker to turn south." Amos pulled rein and spoke to the detail.

"What is this place?" Parks surveyed the mounds and boulders rising from the plain.

"No one knows," Amos said. "Some figure it was Indians who lived here a long time back. But I know it only as a trail marker that leads you to the Canadian River."

At the far western edge of the ancient city,

thousands of gray mounds shimmered like a mirage on the horizon.

"What are those?" Free pointed west.

Amos stared into the glare of the sun and wiped his forehead. "I've been through here a hundred times and never seen that on this prairie. But the flatness of this land will deceive a man. Those may be rocks five hundred yards away."

As the men turned their horses south, the constant northwest breeze gusted and brought with it a sickening smell. The odor slammed into each of the men's nostrils then stomachs and alerted them that something dead was downwind of them.

Free pulled the bandana from around his neck and covered his nose and mouth. He pinched the cloth against his nostrils in the hope that he might fend off the onslaught of nausea overpowering his insides.

Amos stared to the west and tried to make out the shapes rising above the short prairie grasses. "I best go take a look," he said with little enthusiasm.

A tense silence filled the plain, and then Free clucked at Spirit. "We best all go."

The detail turned back west and rode with reluctance toward the humps. Free tightened his bandana and gulped air through his mouth in an attempt to buffer the rotting smell.

A short distance away, the mounds came into focus and Free realized he was looking at thousands of skinned buffalo carcasses. The dead bodies stretched as far as the eye could see and dotted the prairie in varied shades of gray. The scene filled each man in the detail with a vile distaste for those who could perpetrate such an atrocity on the land.

As many as twenty turkey vultures sat with wings outstretched next to each carcass. The scavengers guarded their treasures and seemed content to drink in the powerful smell of death. A frantic hum buzzed above the carcasses and swarms of flies darkened the air.

"My God!" Amos Chapman exclaimed and dry heaved over his horse.

One of the soldiers drew his revolver and fired at a pack of scavengers nearest him. The birds, unable to fly due to the weight in their bellies, scattered to the north in a waddle.

"Forget it, son!" Free hollered. "There are too many of them!"

Parks glanced over to Free. "I think we just found the reason the Southern tribes are ready to go on the warpath."

Free surveyed the prairie and shook his head in disgust. "What a waste," he muttered.

"Let's get out of here!" Parks hollered to Amos.

"Not just yet." Amos lifted his head and pointed fifty yards to the northwest "Look over there," his voice quivered with dread.

Dutch ovens, frying pans, bedding, flour, sugar and clothing littered the prairie and formed a trail that ended at two wagons laden with buffalo hides. Free circled the nearest wagon and found two buffalo hunters tied with rawhide to the spokes of the wheels. Both men were scalped, and their bodies held a dozen Comanche arrows.

Free held his gaze on the men and then turned to Amos. "I reckon this confirms what we feared," he said.

Amos dismounted and searched the ground around the bodies. "There's not a spent cartridge around these men." He pushed his hat back and exhaled softly.

Free looked at the scout, puzzled. "They didn't have any ammunition?"

Amos reached into the uncovered wagon and patted the stack of hides. "Oh, they had ammo; they just used it all on these."

Parks took a quick survey around the prairie and then stepped down from Horse. "You figure they used up all their cartridges and then skinned their kill before making reloads?"

"These two wouldn't be the first to die on this land for a measly twelve bits a hide." Amos walked over to the first man and cut his bindings. "Most likely they won't be the last, either."

"Seems to me that the trail a man rides toward easy money is always filled with prairie dog holes." Free shook his head, sickened by the gruesome scene.

"They didn't even get to their *bite*." Amos pulled a Big Fifty cartridge from the shirt pocket of one of the men.

Parks moved close to Amos and studied the cartridge. "Their bite?"

Amos placed the bullet back into the dead man's pocket. "Every hunter I know, understands what happens if the Comanche catches him past the Cimarron hunting buffalo. They keep one cartridge filled with cyanide for that circumstance."

Parks shook his head and stared grimly at the corpses. "A guaranteed quick death."

"And Comanche won't mutilate a man they don't kill."

Free stared at the wagons. "How come the Comanche didn't take the hides?"

Amos cut the rawhide on the second hunter and said, "Bad medicine. I'll bet my hat that Esa-tai gave the war party a stern warning on removing any of the killed buffalo from this land."

"Esa-tai?" Free asked.

"He's the chief medicine man for the Kwa-hada's. He supposedly holds powerful medicine and is in Quanah's favor presently."

Parks looked back to the southwest. "We best get these men in the ground and make our way to Adobe Walls."

Amos nodded grimly. "The Comanche won't be satisfied with just these two. They've never held with tradition like the Kiowa, so for the Comanche to perform the sun dance means they are asking the Great Spirit for powerful medicine."

"How powerful?" Free asked.

"I figure they want enough medicine to kill every buffalo hunter from Kansas to Texas," Amos replied grimly. "Most likely, their next stop is Adobe Walls."

Chapter Four

The Medicine Lodge, Elk Creek, June 1874

At dusk, on the eve of the sun dance ceremony, the assembled chiefs of the southern plains sat around a fire pit inside the medicine lodge on Elk Creek. The thin brush walls of the lodge covered a frame of cottonwood and cedar. The summer sky moved from east to west across the partially opened roof. The lodge floor contained a layer of clean river sand carried in small pouches by Comanche squaws and spread to a depth of six inches for the sun dancers. Bundles of white sage burned in the fire and created billows of incense that spiraled skyward.

The Comanche, represented by He-Bear, Quanah, and Tabananaka called for the sun dance and sat with their backs to the west. The Kiowa delegation of White Horse, Lone Wolf, Big Bow, and Maman-ti sat to the south. The Cheyenne chiefs, Stone Calf, Minimic and Red Moon, who held allegiance with the Comanche, sat north of the fire.

Esa-tai squatted in the center of the lodge with his back to the east and fanned the white sage smoke with a cedar branch. Behind him, eight less prominent medicine men beat on drums stretched with skinned buffalo hide. As the smoke swirled through the opening of the lodge, Esa-tai began a soft chant.

Oh Great Spirit,
Make my medicine strong.
Oh Great Father,
Consider my plea.
That the buffalo will remain in the land,
And The People will multiply on the earth.

As he finished the first chant, Esa-tai went silent and began to sway side-to-side in rhythm with the drumbeat. After several minutes, the drumbeat became quicker and Esa-tai began to chant once more.

Thank you, Great Father
for your pity on The People.
Thank you for sharp lances
and arrows of true aim.
Great Spirit, have pity.

When the chant ended, Esa-ti stared upward in a trance. Suddenly, the Kwahada medicine man leapt to his feet and stretched his arms upward. Esa-tai closed his eyes and began a series of whoops, "Rah, Rah, Rah." He called to the sky and placed his arms behind his back. "Rah! Rah! Rah!" The whoops became louder. He pushed his left arm skyward, and to the astonishment of the great chiefs, an arrow appeared in his fist. "Rah! Rah! Rah!" Esa-tai screamed and threw up his right arm. A second arrow appeared in his right fist. Esa-tai shook the arrows toward the sky and resumed his chant.

Thank you Great Spirit
for the medicine arrows.

This medicine will protect
The People and drive the
killers of buffalo out
of the land.
Thank you Great Father.

Esa-tai looked to the west and shook both arrows toward his fellow Kwahada. "Power to the Numa!" he chanted the Comanche name. He turned to the south and shook both arrows toward the Kiowa. "Power to the Kiowa!" he chanted. He then turned to the north and shook the arrows at the Cheyenne. "Power to the Cheyenne!" he chanted. He repeated the ceremony twice more and then squatted in the sand.

Quanah nodded confidently and spoke to the chiefs, "This is a strong warrior who gives us all a gift from the Great Spirit."

A great fervor filled the smoke laden lodge and the Comanche and Cheyenne chiefs rocked forward in joy of the shaman's pronouncements.

White Horse frowned, "I do not trust the Wolf Prophet's medicine, and I see many tears flowing from the People if they do as he bids." White Horse remained motionless and kept his arms folded across his chest.

Esa-tai shook both arrows at White Horse. "The great chief Quanah will tell you I hold the medicine of the wolf. And the Great Spirit has directed me through a wolf's dream that the white buffalo hunters will die in their sleep."

Quanah, Tabananaka, and He Bear all jumped to their feet and called the name of Esa-tai's power. "*Puha!*" They shouted. "*Puha!*"

Maman-ti tensed and pointed his index finger

at the heavens. "Esa-tai's *puha* is weak. The Comanche have not followed the Great Spirit's direction as to preparation for the sun dance."

Esa-tai grinned deviously at the Owl Prophet. "Maman-ti cannot speak of the Comanche sun dance. What we do is our custom. The Great Spirit provides Esa-tai with paint that will turn away the buffalo hunter's copper. My medicine is very strong!" The Wolf Prophet sprang to his feet and howled at the slender summer moon.

Quanah looked at the Cheyenne chiefs. "Will you ride with Quanah?"

Stone Calf rose and nodded. "The Cheyenne will hold with their Comanche brothers."

Quanah turned to the Kiowa. "And you Lone Wolf, do you speak for the Kiowa or follow the peace wishes of Kicking Bird. How do you say?"

Lone Wolf stared at his old friend, Maman-ti and then turned to Quanah. "The *ta-'ka-i* never seem to have enough. Never enough land, never enough buffalo, and never enough Kiowa dead. The hunters now mock the People and leave many buffalo scattered across all our lands. I cannot speak for all Kiowa, but Lone Wolf will ride with Quanah."

Maman-ti stood and addressed the chiefs. "Be careful my brothers. The Wolf Prophet shows great hate for the hide hunters, but his hate will only weaken the People. His hate will not hurt the hide hunters. The Owl Prophet will not battle with the whites until the Kiowa complete their sun dance. *Then* the Great Father will show pity for his People."

White Horse stood and held both hands skyward. "I ask Quanah and the Comanche to leave the buffalo hunters for now. Much harm will come to all of our People if we go to war without the Great Spirit's blessing."

Esa-tai frowned at the Kiowa. "Harrumph," he uttered.

Big Bow stood and followed Maman-ti and White Horse as they exited the lodge in silence.

Esa-tai howled at the three as they departed and signaled for the drummers to resume the cadence. As the beat began, Esa-tai began to dance in a series of shuffles and hops. After circling the lodge in an ever-widening arc, he looked at the assembled chiefs and said, "The Great Spirit demands that no skunk or rabbit be killed by the raiding party. Tell your warriors of this demand and make sure the Great Spirit is honored."

The beat of the drums now became more frantic. Quanah glanced upward. The moon's horns faced east. "When the new moon finishes its journey across the sky, The People will ride to the Adobe Walls and kill all the hide hunters!" he screamed.

Chapter Five

Adobe Walls, Texas, June 1874

On a small hill east of Bent Creek, a mile or so from old Fort Adobe, sat the Adobe Walls outpost. The settlement was slightly north of the Canadian River and surrounded by lowland. "Dobe Walls," as the buffalo hunters called it, ran for seven hundred feet from north to south and consisted of four unsightly structures.

The Myer and Leonard Mercantile sat on the north end of the trading post, protected by a picket stockade and fortified by thick walls of dirt. Next door, although a good fifty yards away, was Hanrahan's Saloon with O'Keefe's blacksmith shop next in line. Charles Rath's establishment lay at the south end of the primitive settlement and consisted of a hide yard, restaurant, and store.

At dusk on June 25, the detail from Camp Supply rode into The Walls. As they approached the noise and lights coming from Hanrahan's Saloon they called out a customary hello.

"Who is it?" One of the figures outside of Hanrahan's called back.

"Amos Chapman and a detail from Camp Supply."

Amos?" a voice hollered into the dusk.

"One and the same, Billy," Amos shouted back. "We've come tired and hungry, and with bad news from northeast of here."

"Come in!" Billy Dixon walked toward the approaching horses. "Have a drink of your liking," he offered.

The men stood outside of Hanrahan's later that evening and enjoyed coffee and whiskey. Amos spoke with Billy Dixon, as Fred Leonard, James Hanrahan, Bermuda Carlisle, Andy Johnson, and Bat Masterson listened in.

"Billy, meet my friends and the best horsemen on the southern plains, Free Anderson and Parks Scott."

"You two must be ace-high. I can't remember Amos carrying on so," Billy laughed. "Welcome to the Walls!"

Free took in the figure of Billy Dixon. The slender hunter had a head of long curly hair and his youthful face bore a full bushy mustache that drooped slightly from his upper lip. "Thank you," he said, "We are grateful to find everyone above ground and keeping a full head of hair."

Fred Leonard joined in, "You won't need to worry much about these boys. They all have a wealth of experience fighting Cheyenne. I 'spect you'll find them more than ready for a skirmish."

Free dipped into the neck of his shirt and removed a leather tobacco pouch. "I would never doubt the staunchness of the men here, sir." Free cut an end from his tobacco plug and poked it into his jaw. "I only spoke to my relief in finding all parties enjoying the June heat."

Bermuda Carlisle tossed back a shot of whiskey and spoke in a quiet voice, "In the past week, we've heard that several hunters have been attacked by these savages. Friends of ours now lay scalped and mutilated. I would say, sir, we are all red hot for a fight with these devils."

A murmuring of agreement drifted among the group of hunters and merchants.

Fred Leonard nodded and said, "As you gentlemen can rightly see, this bunch will not let savages scare them away. A good many of us have left stakes in Dodge City and come here to make our fortunes. We all understand the risk that comes with that fortune."

"We came across two of your tradesman dead and scalped near the old city," Free said matter-of-factly. He sipped from a tin of black coffee."

"Two men?" Billy Dixon frowned and looked toward Fred Leonard.

"They were tied to a wagon filled with hides." Free tossed a gaze at Leonard, "That fortune you speak of is probably not so important to those men right now, Mr. Leonard."

Fred Leonard put a hand above his upper lip and wiped his mouth. He looked inside Hanrahan's and listened to the hunters inside laughing and telling long tales. "That had to be Freeman and Morton," he uttered.

Billy Dixon nodded his head. "They were bound and determined to hunt that northeast prairie, just the two of them."

Amos tossed the remainder of his coffee to the ground and held the cup toward Bermuda Carlisle. "Could you spare a pinch of that whiskey?"

The grizzled hunter poured a generous amount for the scout. He grinned, "That's what I like, a man who partakes no matter the difficulty and remains un-a-feared of a few savages on the loose."

Amos took a long sip from the cup and looked

into Billy Dixon's eyes. "Appears to be more than a few raiding parties, Billy. The Comanche are on Elk Creek holding a sun dance."

"What?" Billy blurted. "Are you sure?"

"Lieutenant Baldwin sent me here to warn all of you that three hundred Cheyenne left the reservation a week ago. They headed to Elk Creek to join with the Comanche. I figure it's going to get bad, Billy."

"A Comanche sun dance?" Dixon considered the notion. "Why would they call a sun dance, the Comanche have never held for ceremony."

Free looked at Amos and then turned his attention to Billy Dixon, "I reckon they're as determined as you men to protect their fortune."

"Huh?" Dixon glanced up at Free. "Their fortune?"

"Buffalo. Seems you both covet the same fortune and I figure each is determined to kill the other for it."

The circle of men threw hard gazes at Free.

"What's that supposed to mean?" Fred Leonard shouted. "You ride into The Walls on a marked Kiowa pony and a bee in your bonnet about killing buffalo? I can tell you right away Cowboy, you're just barking at a knot with this crowd!"

Parks, stepped forward, placed his hand on Free's shoulder, and said to the others, "It's been a long several days for us," he said, "We're going to catch some rest."

Free recognized Park's grip on his shoulder. It was a signal to be silent and he knew to forgo any talk about who held rights to the buffalo. "Gentlemen," he tipped his hat and they started to leave.

Amos tapped the tin cup against his thigh and

exhaled softly, "We didn't ride here to tell you men how to run your camp. We rode here to deliver a message from Lieutenant Baldwin. And we've done that. I would ask you consider what you've heard here tonight and make your own decisions as to staying or leaving."

Bat Masterson, quiet throughout, broke his silence, "And we thank you all for bringing that message. You rode through some dangerous country to get here. But I'm not leaving. I've sat around for weeks waiting on the herd's arrival, and now that they're here, it seems foolish to cut and run."

Billy Dixon stared out at his wagon and then looked back at the assembled hunters from inside the saloon. "Bat's right. Amos and these men undertook a dangerous ride to come here and warn us. Let's all sleep on this tonight."

Amos moved forward and shook Billy's hand, "That's all I ask. We'll bunk out near your wagon if that's OK. My orders are to return to Camp Supply after advising you of the situation at Elk Creek. Any man who wishes, can ride with us in the morning."

Chapter Six

Adobe Walls, Texas, June 1874

Free grabbed his Mexican saddle by the biscuit and tossed the rig across Spirit's back. He reached under the mustang and pulled the cinch tight. He let his thoughts drift to his wife, Clara, and his son, William Parks. He looked over Spirit's back and tossed a gaze at Parks, then showed a wide smile.

"What's got you grinning like a fox in the henhouse, Free?" Parks smoothed his saddle blanket and cast a crooked smile.

"I was just thinking of your namesake." Free laughed, "I can picture him running to the corral this morning, ready to feed the mustangs and Clara . . ."

". . . running behind hollering for him to wait for her," Parks interjected.

"Right," Free laughed harder. "But does he listen to his mother?"

"Of course not." Parks squared his saddle on Horse's back. "He's got too much of his father in him."

Free cinched the girth belt and dropped his stirrups. "What are you trying to say, Parks?"

"I'm only saying . . ."

"Free. Parks." Amos Chapman approached from behind and walked the grulla mustang between the two men. "I guess I've jawed here all

I can. The men and I are riding back to Camp Supply."

"Alone?" Free looked down the empty street.

"Appears so. I reckon these hunters are a might too prideful to pull up stakes now, what with the buffalo moving into the Panhandle."

Free turned away from Spirit and extended his hand toward the scout. "Well, no one can say you didn't try to warn them, Amos. Good luck to you and ride safe."

Parks walked around Horse and approached the detail. "Take care, Amos. I hope you fare well in your future endeavors."

"Thanks, Parks." The scout raised his hand and motioned for the detail to move out. "I'll be sure and get your money on the next supply train to Fort Griffin."

The military detail gigged their mounts and galloped toward the Adobe Walls Creek. In a matter of minutes, the group became dark specks on the prairie.

"I reckon we best fill our canteens and packs before we pull foot." Free slipped the reins over Spirit's head.

Parks studied the sun and nodded his agreement. "I reckon that to be a sound idea. Mr. Leonard should have everything we need."

A half hour later, Free strode from the well situated between Leonard's store and Hanrahan's. The tall, muscular mustanger carried two canteens and a buffalo bladder filled with water.

Parks had secured a bag of flour, and tossed it behind his saddle, securing it with rawhide keeper straps.

"I've got the water," Free called out.

"Good." Parks looked at his friend and placed hardtack and smoked beef in his saddle pack. "As hot as that sun is today, we're going to need plenty of it."

Free strode out to Spirit and stepped into the stirrup.

"Free! Parks! Hold on there!" a voice boomed from Hanrahan's.

Free turned in the saddle and watched Billy Dixon hurry from the saloon with Bat Masterson on his heels.

"Morning, Billy." Parks tipped his hat, "Bat."

Free pulled the left rein and turned Spirit to face the two men. "Morning," he nodded.

Parks walked Horse up even with Free and looked at the approaching men with a careful eye. "I've got a bad feeling we're fixing to be asked for a favor," he whispered.

Billy stood in front of Spirit and rubbed the pony's nose. "I need to ask a favor." He looked at Free and then over to Parks.

"What is it you're needing, Billy?" Free reached for the tobacco pouch hanging from his neck and removed a small plug.

"I know you two are set on leaving this morning, but the boys and I got to talking and we reckon we owe it to Freeman and Morton to bring their worked hides back here to sell. You know, so we can give their families the money they deserve."

"So what's the favor?" Parks looked down at the hunter and rubbed his chin.

Billy glanced up at Parks and squared his jaw. "We need for you to lead us out to where you buried those men."

Free took a sidelong glance at the hunter. "That's a good half day's ride from here," he stated.

"I know. I know it's asking a lot from you both, but wouldn't you want the same if it were you lying in the bone orchard?"

Parks tilted his hat back and leaned forward on his saddle. "Billy, I don't know if you heard what Amos said last night, but this country is a dangerous place for men to be caught out on the open prairie."

The young buffalo hunter turned to Parks, "I know, Parks, but me and the boys are determined to go. The Shadler brothers rode in today but are willing to go back out with a team of their oxen and haul back Freeman's wagon . . ."

"Why do you need us, Billy? Free interrupted, confused. "You men know this country better than us."

"That we do, Free, but truth be told we all *know* that horse of yours is protected by the Kiowa. There's not an Indian on the Panhandle Plains who'll risk angering the Great Spirit by spilling blood near that pony. It would sure make the journey safer for us if you and Parks were to guide us to those boys' wagon."

Free leaned toward Parks and handed him a cut of tobacco. "What do you think?"

Parks scratched his head and stared northward. "We might be fixing to step off into some deep water if we get involved, Free," he cautioned.

Free tightened his lips, "I reckon that's so, but my gut tells me I should help. Those men's families certainly deserve the hide money." He turned back to the buffalo hunter. "I'll take you boys out there, Billy."

Billy grinned and wheeled toward the saloon. "You won't regret this." He called over his shoulder, "I promise we'll go out, fetch that wagon, and then get you both back on the trail in double-quick time."

Parks surveyed the surrounding countryside and then looked over to Free, "I've got a bad feeling in my bones on this one, Free."

Free saw the concern in his friend's eyes and knew better than to ignore Park's foreboding. His intuition had saved their hides more than once. "We'll take them out and be back here by mid-afternoon," he offered as reassurance.

Parks poked the tobacco plug deep into his jaw and spit onto the dusty street. "I just hope we haven't hopped on an Indian broke horse, Free, because you can darn well bet every Kiowa for a hundred miles will be watching us."

Chapter Seven

Adobe Walls Creek, Texas, June 1874

Quanah and the war party of the Southern Plains Indians rode from Elk Creek after the new moon crossed the summer sky. The column of several hundred mounted warriors stretched for a mile across the landscape and rode in organized bands of fifteen to twenty men. Each warrior held a string of ponies for the purpose of fresh mounts. In the late afternoon, the group arrived at a stand of cottonwood trees near Adobe Walls Creek.

As long shadows crept across the land, Esa-tai called for council, and the warrior chiefs assembled in a small depression below the crest of Skunk Ridge under the cooling shade of the cottonwood canopy. The assembled delegation sat in a semi-circle around the Comanche medicine man and waited patiently as Esa-tai closed his eyes and began to chant softly.

After several minutes, Esa-tai opened his eyes and greeted the assembly, "Warriors. Last night the spirit wolf came to me in a dream. He held a sleeping white child in his mouth and on his back rode the hawk and the snake."

The chiefs nodded and rocked back and forth murmuring a soft chant.

Quanah brimmed with confidence and asked, "What does your dream mean, Wolf Prophet?"

Esa-tai jumped to his feet. "The wolf brings good news! The hide hunters will all be asleep when The People come down upon them like hawks from the sky! With their rifles all stacked against the walls of their shelters, The People will strike like the snake and take their lives!"

Quanah slapped his thighs loudly and turned to his fellow warrior chiefs, "So it is said; so it will be."

Esa-tai invited the chiefs to rise. "Go back to your bands and tell your braves to paint their bodies in red and yellow only. The ponies must be painted in the same colors."

The group nodded their understanding and encircled the Wolf Prophet.

Esa-tai untied a buffalo sac from around his waist and dipped his hand into the pouch. "Mix your war paint with Esa-tai's *puha*." The Wolf Prophet dropped a handful of dirt into the cupped hands of each chief. "This will keep any white bullets from penetrating your skin."

As Lone Wolf walked back to the Kiowa bands, a warrior known as Little Boy ran to his side and walked with the chief.

"What is it, Little Boy?"

"Lone Wolf, I rode the northern prairie looking for soldiers as you asked."

"Were any of the blue coats near the Adobe Walls?"

"No, not one soldier. But I did see a wagon loaded with *aungaupi* crossing the land. The wagon traveled toward the Adobe Walls."

"Good! They will die with their friends!"

"The wagon was led by two men," Little Boy

continued, "And one rode the spirit *tséeyñ* of White Horse."

Lone Wolf stopped abruptly. "Are you sure it is a spirit pony, Little Boy?"

"I looked through the long glass, Lone Wolf. It was the *tséeyñ* given to the buffalo man."

"*Aungaupi chi*?" Lone Wolf asked excitedly.

"It was *aungaupi chi*."

"So the buffalo man takes a side!" Lone Wolf spoke loudly, "So be it; he will die in the Adobe Walls with the hide hunters!"

Little Boy nodded in understanding.

"One thing, Little Boy."

"Yes, Lone Wolf."

"When the battle begins, you must ride to the hunters' pens and take the spirit horse. We must not disrespect the Great Spirit by allowing a Kiowa *tséeyñ* to die with the whites."

Little Boy clenched his right hand into a fist. "It is done, Lone Wolf."

Chapter Eight

Adobe Walls, Texas, June 1874

The whoosh of Ike Shadler's whip preceded a loud crack that snapped Free's attention away from two figures silhouetted against the southeast skyline.

"Gettt uppp!" Ike sung to the team of oxen.

The massive animals plodded across the prairie pulling the recovered Freeman and Morton wagon in a symphony of creaks and groans. The wagon's retrieval had turned into one difficulty after another for the men. When they arrived at the site, Ike inspected the wagon and informed the group it wouldn't pull half a mile if the wheels weren't greased. The chore of removing all four wheels kept the men exposed on the plains for two extra hours and rankled Free about his decision to help the hunters.

"Friends of yours?" Parks swung around in the saddle and glanced at the pair who slowly trailed the wagon's progress.

"Couldn't say. You suppose they're Kiowa?"

Parks glanced back again. "Hard to know. But more than likely a scouting party for one of the tribes."

"I *guess* we should have ridden on this morning," Free said, anguished.

Parks pushed a chaw of tobacco into his jaw.

"Don't be so hard on yourself, Free. A man without some fuss in his life each day gets satisfied. And after a time, he's sleeping on feathers and washing his face from a bowl," he joked.

"I think you and I will be OK then." Free smiled back then glanced at the moon visible in the day sky. "Looks like we'll have a full moon to ride under tonight."

Parks cut a glance back to their trackers. "With Indians about, it might be best not to ride out tonight. That moon will make us easy targets for a Comanche or Kiowa arrow."

"Even with Spirit?"

"Our friends back there have watched us freight hides toward Adobe Walls. I reckon Spirit won't be much good to us anymore."

Free's face slackened as Park's words settled in his mind. "I 'spect that's true." he said.

As the last parcel of daylight streaked across the sky, a charcoal outline of buildings rose in the distance.

Appears we'll be staying Saturday night in Adobe Walls." Parks said, "I just hope it's not one night too many."

In the early hours of Sunday morning, the call from two owls drifted from Adobe Walls Creek. Unable to sleep, his thoughts consumed with Clara and William Parks, Free sat up and listened to nature's orchestra. Under the full moon, night birds, frogs, and locusts provided a backdrop for the owls and affirmed all was right on the Panhandle Plains.

Spirit grazed on grass shoots nearby, but

appeared disturbed by both the sounds and the oppressive heat. The restless mustang kept his head low to the ground and inhaled loudly as he searched for young seed head. He snorted at each owl's screech and shook his back violently in response. In the distance, Horse rolled on his back and scattered dust in the breezeless night. Free appraised the camp and decided he better get some shut-eye before sunrise. He laid his head against the saddle and rested his hat on his face when a thunderous crack jolted him upright. He leapt from the ground and instinctively jerked the Colt from his holster. Barefoot and shirtless, he searched the camp for any sign of gunfire and then heard a commotion from inside Hanrahan's saloon.

"What is it?" Parks woke with a start and sprang to his feet.

"I don't know, but it sounded like a .44 Sharps went off next to me," Free answered.

The men put an ear into the air as a strange quiet descended on The Walls, and then a voice hollered from Hanrahan's, "The lodge poles cracked! We're gonna need some help in here afore this roof comes down on us!"

Free and Parks raced into the saloon. The hunters who chose to sleep inside were looking at the massive hewn cottonwood trunk supporting the sod roof.

"What's going on?" Free shouted.

Jim Hanrahan looked at Free and Parks, "The support pole has cracked. We're going to need to fix a prop or this whole roof will collapse!"

Several hours later, two eight-inch diameter cottonwoods supported the cracked ridge pole. As the weary hunters moved back toward their bedding, the dim light of day flashed on the eastern horizon.

"I swear it was rifle fire that brought us all to our feet," Free said, confused.

"Why would Hanrahan make up a story about the ridge pole snapping? That doesn't make much sense," Parks said.

"I don't know, but maybe it's for the best. Let's saddle up and cut a path."

Parks yawned at the orange streaks illuminating the sky, announcing the morning. "Might as well, we're up anyway." He lifted his saddle from the ground and whistled for Horse.

Free walked to Spirit and lifted the reins that dragged the ground beneath the mustang. "Come on, Spirit. It's time we got on our way."

Billy Dixon leaned against his wagon and tossed a bedroll behind the lazy board. The young hunter looked over at Free and Parks. "You two leaving us?" he asked.

"I think we've been here long enough, Billy," Free smiled.

"Well, thanks again for your help yesterday and this morning." He nodded toward Hanrahan's.

Parks cinched the girth strap on Horse and caught a blur of movement from the corner of his eye. A man, hat in hand, raced toward them, from the Adobe Walls Creek. "Who or what is that, Billy?" he asked.

The young hide hunter set his eyes on the figure and squinted. "Looks to be Billy Ogg. I sent him to the creek to fetch my horses."

Free cocked his head and tried to discern the darkness boiling over the horizon. "Looks like a herd of buffalo trailing him."

Parks pulled a pair of field glasses from his saddle pack and looked into the distance. "Best pony up for Hanrahan's boys! It appears every Indian on the Southern plains is hot after Billy Ogg!"

Chapter Nine

Adobe Walls, Texas, June 1874

Billy Ogg reached Hanrahan's completely exhausted and collapsed face down in the dirt. From behind, the howl of *Eeeeeeee-YUH-haaeeeetaaaaheh* rumbled across the prairie like summer thunder. Billy pushed his hat onto his head and pulled the brim down over his ears in an attempt to silence the haunting war cry.

The advancing swarm deafened the air to all other sounds, so Billy did not hear the creak of the door in front of him.

A dark-skinned hand eased from the slight opening and grabbed the hunter by his buckskin collar. With a mighty tug, Free yanked the whimpering hunter into the safety of Hanrahan's.

"Praise be!" Billy exclaimed.

Parks stood behind the door and when he saw Billy was safely inside, he pushed his shoulder into the wood planking and slammed it shut to the attacking horde. A barrage of arrows quickly followed and plunked harmlessly against the saloon entrance.

Billy shook uncontrollably. The frightened hunter ran both hands through his hair and patted the top of his head repeatedly. The realization of what lay beyond Hanrahan's door rushed over him and caused his knees to buckle. He placed both palms on the floor to support his body as a wave of fear rushed over him.

Free pulled the juddering hunter to his feet and hollered, "Are you hit anywhere?"

Billy stared at Free for a split second and then uttered, "No, but I ain't never run so far so fast in my life."

Outside, a swarm of warriors reached Hanrahan's and began to pound against the saloon door. The intensity of the Indian's whoops and shouts held the hunters in a fixed pose of fear.

"Sounds like the same yell the rebels used during the war," Parks hollered.

Free looked around Hanrahan's at the paralyzed men and shouted, "Get anything you can to barricade this door! Move! Or we'll find ourselves wall to wall with Indians!"

Shaken from their palsy, a frantic scramble erupted inside the saloon as the men grabbed for tables, chairs, and anything else to act as a barrier between them and the savages outside. They jammed the furniture against the door and piled the crates high on the walls.

Parks stuck his Colt through one of the gun slots and discharged the weapon with random fire while the others worked feverishly to secure the building.

The ping of arrows continued to assail the saloon door and intimidated the harried hunters to stop their work every few seconds and cut a glance at their timber barricade.

"How many of them are there?" Billy Dixon shouted over the rifle fire and thud of bullets that plunked into the sod walls.

"Thousands!" Billy Ogg screamed out.

After a few minutes, the hunters' initial panic faded. With the front door battened, the saloon suddenly seemed defensible and impregnable. Regaining their composure, the men now began to take up arms.

"Did everyone get inside?" Parks asked Billy Dixon.

Billy took a quick inventory of the hunters. "There's ten of us here. I can't speak to who might be at Fred Leonard's or Rath's store."

Outside, a loud cry sounded shrilly. A Comanche chief in full war paint and buffalo headdress sat atop a squat Medicine Hat mustang. The chief's face wore the black paint of death. His pony pranced ceremoniously in front of the four small buildings of The Walls. The chief taunted the hunters with insults and begged them to come out and fight. He carried a fourteen-foot war lance tight against his side and swung the flint tip back and forth menacingly. With no takers to his challenge, he backed his pony against Hanrahan's door and slapped the horse's flank with a leather strap. The mustang kicked repeatedly at the door but with little effect. Unable to gain entrance to the hunters, the chief shouted to the warriors, "Kill everything!"

Free peered out of a gun slot and exhaled loudly. The war party, all painted in yellow and red, raced their ponies around the four buildings whooping and shouting. Calico streamers strung from willow hoops woven into their horse's manes fluttered in the air and the ponies carried the same paint as their riders. Many of the warriors bore buffalo hide shields decorated with feathers of striking colors that flitted at the slightest movement.

The Comanche chief urged on his warriors by remaining in full view of the saloon, defiant to the guns inside. "See, brothers!" he yelled, "The hunters hide in shame for they know the power of Esa-tai's medicine!"

The circling warriors yipped louder at the chief's pronouncement and some braves ventured close enough to the hunter's gun slots to slap them with their palms.

The chief looked around the camp and noticed a wagon readied with a hitched team of oxen. He rode over and poked the war lance through the goods inside.

Suddenly, Ike Shadler sprang from his hiding spot and leveled his Sharps on the chief. He fumbled to cock the rifle and in the split second delay, the chief thrust the lance deep into Ike's chest. Howling at the first kill, the chief pulled the impaled hunter from the wagon. A group of braves looked on as the lanced hunter flopped about on the ground and rushed forward eager to join in the game.

As the enjoined warriors counted a second coup on the dying victim, a chilling scream filled the air. Jacob Shadler leapt from his concealment in the wagon and attempted to make for the safety of Hanrahan's. He covered only a few feet before a fusillade of arrows entered his back.

The black-faced chief smiled and lowered himself from his horse. He raised Ike's lifeless head by the hair and voiced a deep guttural chant. He kept his gaze fixed on the saloon and lifted the scalp with two deft cuts of his knife. He mockingly waved the scalp across his body and once more taunted the hunters to come out and fight.

After several minutes, he tied the scalp to the tip of his lance, jumped on his horse and rode away praising Esa-tai's *puha*.

Billy Dixon stared at the proceedings in disgust and sank against the wall. "That chief in black face paint is Quanah himself," he uttered to the group.

The remaining Comanche dispatched Jacob's scalp quickly and rejoined the other warriors who continued to circle the buildings.

"I'll kill all of you red devils!" Bermuda Carlisle raced for a gun portal, a Big 50 in hand. The emotion-filled hunters joined Bermuda and let their anger boil over in a barrage of bullets from the saloon. After the volley, a smoky haze choked the room and left the men dry mouthed and exhausted.

Parks shouted to the hunters, "Take your time and make your bullets count! If we can put a few rounds in that Comanche chief, Quanah, we might take some wind out of this bunch!"

From across the room, Bat Masterson screamed, "Sweet Jesse! They're killing our horses!"

Free slid next to Masterson and looked outside the narrow portal. The twang of bowstrings resonated on the dusty thoroughfare and arrows darkened the air. Cheyenne, Comanche, and Kiowa warriors were using their bows to shoot the hunters' staked horses.

In front of the Shadlers' wagon, another group fired rifles at close range into the oxen. Free swiveled his head back and forth across the small opening and tried to locate Spirit. After several seconds, he saw the mustang standing calmly next to Billy Dixon's wagon.

"Spirit!" Free shouted, "Over here, boy!"

The mustang's ears perked up at Free's voice and he turned his head toward Hanrahan's.

"Spirit!" Free called again.

The horse snickered and crossed as though invisible through the hundreds of Indian warriors. Ten yards from the saloon, a loop of rope flashed in the air and fell around the mustang's neck. From behind, a Kiowa brave pulled the rope taut and cinched it tightly. With his rope set, the brave kneed his pony behind the shoulder, signaling the horse to back up. Enraged, Spirit whinnied and tugged violently against his captor's rope. The Kiowa brave shouted for help and soon a second rope settled around Spirit's neck. Spirit's eyes widened and he reared against the ropes but the struggle only served to tighten the lassoes and cut off his air.

Free pushed his Colt through the gun slot and fired recklessly at the two Kiowa.

The first brave hearing the report looked toward the saloon and shouted, "Your bullets cannot hurt me! You have chosen sides, *Aungaupi chi*, and for that the Kiowa retake their pony and leave you to die with the other hide hunters!"

With both ropes tightly fixed, the Kiowa spun their ponies and ploddingly began to drag Spirit toward Skunk Ridge. Sensing the futility of resisting, Spirit snorted and reluctantly galloped away with his captors.

"Spirit!" Free screamed.

Parks hurried over to Free's side. "Did you see him?"

"The Kiowa have him."

"What?"

"You were right. They know we helped the hunters recover that wagon."

"Free, catch hold of yourself! We have more difficulty than Spirit does right now! He still carries White Horse's medicine, and no warrior would risk harming him during battle."

Parks looked out the portal and watched as Spirit galloped away from The Walls. "They aim to keep us locked down. Without horses, we're in a tight spot." His thoughts went to Horse, and he issued an ear-piercing whistle through the portal.

Horse stood in a plum thicket fifty yards from the fighting. Upon hearing Park's whistle, he raced toward the sound. As he crossed the whirling circle of Indians, a Comanche warrior spied him and signaled for the others to hold their arrows. As the circle slowed, the brave yipped twice and chased after Horse with a loop of rope.

"Yah! Git outta here, Horse!" Parks screamed and issued a high shrill whistle.

Horse nodded twice and threw his head into the wind. He raced west from the camp with the Comanche brave in hot pursuit.

Chapter Ten

Skunk Ridge, Texas, June 1874

As the mid-morning sun blistered the plains and drove most creatures in search of shade, Quanah moved most of his warriors back to Skunk Ridge, leaving only a few trusted Kwahada to watch the hunters.

The warriors galloped into the camp and announced their victory with dazzling displays of horsemanship. The Cheyenne entered first. Their braves rode backward and hurled curses at Adobe Walls. The young and old warriors of the camp howled in laughter at the Cheyenne feat. The Kiowa followed and sprinted past the camp congregates, standing upright on their ponies. The Comanche entered last and demonstrated why they were called the greatest horsemen on the plains. Each Comanche, secured only by locked ankles, hung below their horse's neck and swung from side to side, only inches from the ground.

Quanah greeted each passing warrior with yips and shouts in praise of their courage. He shook the black-haired scalp adorning his war lance and felt the prophecy of invincibility was indeed true.

Esa-tai, beside Quanah, sat on his horse, chanted and shook his hands skyward as each warrior astride a pony passed by. The Wolf Prophet and his mustang were adorned in yellow mud emanating a mysterious, spirit-like appearance.

"The Great Spirit looks with favor on Esa-tai's medicine, for not one warrior carries a wound from the attack," Quanah praised.

Esa-tai nodded and pointed to Quanah's lance. "This morning the Great Spirit gave the People but a small gift for their prayers, but at the next attack our blessings will be many and the number of scalps on your war lance will grow by twenty."

Quanah curled his upper lip into a wicked smile. "Keep your medicine strong, Wolf Prophet, for after we swoop down on the whites once more, they will come to know the full power of the People. When we have finished here today, I will take all the warriors and go north to rid our land of the whites and their wagons."

The camp buzzed with activity as the multitude of warriors returned. The separate bands reunited and soon laughter and loud storytelling filled the air. Some bands danced while others sang, and many warriors replayed their exploits through hand signals. The Comanche warriors present for the killing of the two hide hunters howled in joy at the coup counted on the white men.

While the Cheyenne, Kiowa, and Comanche relived the morning battle, boys, who had not yet earned their medicine, carried water in buffalo bladders to each band, providing the warriors with a much-needed drink.

After the storytelling quieted, Quanah rode through the bands and urged the warriors to ready themselves. At his bidding, the braves repainted their bodies, switched to their fresh mounts and prepared once more to ride into Adobe Walls.

When all had remounted, Quanah led the war party to the crest of Skunk Ridge. A group of older chiefs sat around a small fire on the exposed ridge. Quanah approached respectfully and announced himself by wiggling his index finger down the middle of his chest.

The group nodded their pleasure with the attack and invited him to sit. He smiled and threw his gaze skyward to observe the sun's position. Happy at the sign, he dismounted and positioned himself on the eastern side of the fire.

"You have fared well," a white-haired chief commented and held out a sacred pipe.

Quanah received the pipe with both hands and took a deep draw of the smoke. "It feels well," he said.

"Go then and finish the battle. Count many coup and bring us the promise of Esa-tai," the chief said.

Quanah nodded to each chief, returned the pipe to the fire and rose. He turned to view the gathered war party awaiting his command. He held his hands toward the sun and began to blow smoke from his mouth. The white plume drifted toward the bands and then disappeared in the air. As the smoke dispersed in the wind, the warriors all yipped loudly and shook their weapons.

Quanah leapt to his mount's back and shouted, "The Wolf Prophet's medicine is strong! Stronger than the hunter's guns!"

The warriors howled with delight at their leader's words.

"I say today is a good day to fight our enemies! As sure as the trees grow tall and the great river runs long, it is our day to be victorious!"

Another great whoop filled Skunk Ridge.

Quanah stabbed his lance into the ground and

signaled for his rifle. A young boy approached on foot and handed the war chief the Winchester.

Quanah grabbed the rifle and began to sing as he rode for Adobe Walls. "Let's ride into the Adobe Walls and kill all the hunters! For that's why the Great Father sent us to this place!"

Chapter Eleven

Adobe Walls, Texas, June 1874

A smothering mixture of charcoal and sulphur lingered in the stale air of Hanrahan's. The acrid cloud hovered head high and caused the men inside to retch in uncontrollable coughing spasms.

The spent gunpowder left a metalic taste on Free's tongue and burned his eyes. He wiped his face with a shirtsleeve and glanced back through the narrow gun slot. The departing war party dispersed in billowing clouds of dust and a majestic show of their horse skills. Some of the warriors sat backward on their ponies and continued to shoot arrows at Hanrahan's door, while others made one more pass around the buildings riding below their steeds' necks.

"They're gone," Free remarked in awe.

"For the time being anyhow." Parks took a deep breath.

Billy Dixon stared up at the ceiling and rubbed his eyes. "I've never seen Indians kill livestock that were easy pickings for stealing."

Parks looked about at his desperate companions. All sat with their backs to the wall displaying the blank stares of whipped men. "Quanah didn't ride in here with a raiding party, Billy. They came with a fixed purpose to kill all of us and make sure every settler in Texas knows of it."

Billy Ogg looked up at Parks, confused by the words he heard. "They're going to set example by us?"

"They shot the horses and oxen to make sure we stay put until they're finished," Parks lamented.

Billy Dixon took his feet and dusted his shirt. "That being so, I'm not obliged to their purpose. What do we need to do to remain above snakes, Parks?"

Free heard the determination in Billy's voice and spoke with his own bravado, "Let's get our cartridges ready then. When Quanah and all of those braves show back up, it will be our turn to welcome them as they did us this morning." The conviction of his words were a much needed inspiration.

Bat Masterson jumped to his feet and added, "That's right boys. This bunch should be easy pickings seeing how they're thicker than flies on a buffalo's back."

Parks smiled at the renewed confidence of the men. "You boys all heard what that Kiowa shouted at Free . . . they think the Great Spirit has granted them invincibility. Billy, Bat, Bermuda . . . you boys can hit a buffalo at half a mile. Let's dust a few of those Indians off their ponies on the next charge and you can believe we'll have them doubting their medicine."

Billy Dixon lifted his Sharps from against the wall. "I'll need to make my way to Rath's. I have a case of ammo sitting there and I aim to take part in this hunt. I won't die indoors without cartridges."

Jim Hanrahan stood and walked to Billy's side. "I'll go with you and help bring another case for the rest of us. If Parks is right, we might sit here a 'spell."

"All right, but the two of you best keep your eyes skinned," Free said. "I reckon Quanah left a few scouts behind waiting to ambush any of us venturing outdoors."

Both men nodded at Free.

Free held silent for a minute and then looked over at Parks, "OK. Good luck to the both of you."

Billy and Hanrahan nodded and moved to the saloon door.

"We're ready," Billy said.

Parks cracked the door, looked left, then right and both men exited the saloon. Outside, Billy crouched low and sprinted toward Rath's with Jim Hanrahan close on his heels.

Midway to Rath's, a Comanche war cry broke the still of the day and a dozen bullets followed. Billy and Hanrahan stopped for a second, regained their nerve, and raced for Rath's dodging lead as they went.

Free rushed to the gun slot at the first shout and quickly looked toward Rath's store.

"Are they OK?" Parks called out.

"Those boys are fine," Free answered. He then turned his attention to a blur on the horizon. "But I figure we better make ready! Seems Quanah and his bunch are riding back to finish us!"

Chapter Twelve

Adobe Walls, Texas, June 1874

Quanah kneed his pony to a stop five hundred yards from Adobe Walls and raised his right hand signaling for the herd of warriors behind him to halt. His face, a terrifying mask, freshly painted in black from forehead to chin, embodied death. Bright alternating stripes of red and yellow ran the length of his body and Ike Shadler's scalp, now tied to his rifle barrel, fluttered in the June breeze.

"There is no need to circle the hide hunters!" he called out confidently. "Their copper bullets are useless against The People!"

The front line of warriors raised their weapons in a great whoop.

"We will charge straight away and knock down their doors and shoot through their small windows until they beg us for their lives." Quanah pointed to Rath's store. "Stone Calf, take your warriors there!"

The Cheyenne chief nodded and motioned his warriors to follow him to the far left of the war column.

Quanah watched the Cheyenne position their horses and then pointed to Myers and Leonard's store, "Lone Wolf, let the Kiowa kill the hunters there!"

Lone Wolf looked at the picketed store and shouted to his warriors.

Quanah motioned the Winchester toward Hanrahan's saloon, "The Comanche will kill all inside the whiskey house!"

More whoops and yips followed.

Quanah looked at both ends of his war line, kicked his pony's flank, and raced headlong for Hanrahan's while firing his Winchester repeatedly at the sod walls of the saloon. His high-pitched wail of, *"Rah! Rah! Rah!"* accompanied the bullets and urged the great surge of warriors forward. A fifteen-foot length of rein encircled his midsection, a precaution in the event he lost contact with his pony.

Four hundred yards from the saloon, his prized mustang stumbled, dipped forward and collapsed on the dry crusted earth sending a cloud of dust high into the air. Crumpled, the mustang screamed out with a loud whinny as he tried desperately to regain his feet.

Quanah jerked forward and somersaulted over the mustang's neck in a series of rolls. He bounced several yards from the downed steed, chucked out in a whirl of earth and confusion.

Regaining his bearings, he grabbed the rein still tied to his waist and made his way hand-over-hand down the braided leather rope. He figured a prairie dog burrow felled the horse. Such holes pockmarked the prairie near Adobe Walls.

Tugging at the rein, he shouted for the pony to get up and struggled to lift the animal's head. Feeling only dead weight, he dropped to his knees and looked into the horse's lifeless glazed eyes. He searched the mustang's chest and found a bullet hole running blood. In great confusion, he stood and looked at his warriors, wondering if one of them had shot his horse mistakenly.

As he tried to make sense of the unfolding scene, small swirls of dust were kicked up by his feet. Quanah realized the hide hunters were shooting the long rifles at him and he scrambled for a rotting buffalo carcass nearby. As he dove behind the carcass, a burning sensation tore into his side and caused him to roll backward. Seconds later, he felt a stabbing pain that he knew could only be a bullet's bite. Realizing his cover was useless, he crawled back to his dead horse and sought protection from the gunfire erupting around him.

Quanah gazed over his dead pony and listened to the sporadic but deadly sound of the hide hunters' long rifles. From both ends of the battle, warriors dropped one and then another from their ponies. During the great killing confusion, Quanah dropped his head and wondered the cause of such betrayal.

"What have we done?" he screamed at the sky. "Why have you left us?"

From the south, a pony raced for him, and the Comanche warrior, Toyarohco, held an outstretched arm.

Quanah caught Toyarohco's arm and pulled himself up on the Comanche pony. In seconds, he was spirited away to Skunk Ridge.

Chapter Thirteen

Adobe Walls, Texas, June 1874

Ihit that red devil!" Bermuda Carlisle shouted.

Free eyed the departing raiders and breathed out in relief. His lungs burned from the stifling cloud of gunpowder that blanketed the entire room.

Unable to tolerate the suffocating dust any longer, he pulled the oak door open to the sweltering heat of the day.

"Hey!" Bermuda cried out, "Whataya think you're doing?"

Parks held a hand up to the grizzled hide hunter and followed Free outside.

"You OK?"

Free stooped and placed both palms on his knees. "I'm fine. I just needed a fresh breath."

Parks surveyed the ghastly scene in front of them. Dead horses and oxen littered the land from one end of the Walls to the other.

He had not seen such carnage on a battlefield since the Civil War.

Ike and Jacob Shadler lay within twenty yards of the saloon curled in the rigid grip of death, their eyes opened and focused on the sun. "We're going to need to bury those boys before the day gets longer," he said stoically.

Free looked up and gazed at the carnage across

the dirt road. "You think those braves are going to stay gone for awhile?"

Parks chewed on his bottom lip. "I reckon they're going to hold council and try to figure out what medicine we're holding."

Free straightened and turned toward his friend. "I suppose that's so. Still, I don't like our situation. With the horses all dead or run-off we're left riding shank's mare."

"Horse should be within whistling range." Parks gazed to the West.

"I guess I should have refused those boys the favor yesterday," Free said, ruefully. "Cause if I had, then we'd both be a day closer to home right now. I hate leaving Clara and William Parks for so long."

Parks produced a half smile, "Just fuss, Free. What would our lives be without it?"

"Everybody make it out OK?" Billy Dixon's voice shouted from Rath's.

Slowly men made their way from the protection of the individual buildings and into the street.

"All right, here," Bat Masterson said as he exited Hanrahan's and strode up to Free and Parks.

"We're all OK," Fred Leonard called walking trance-like from his store.

Free looked at the emerging men and felt a smile at the corners of his mouth. "We did good," he called out.

Billy Dixon walked up the street slapping his hat against his thigh. A cloud of dust flew from his pants with each swat. "Thank the Lord for sod walls and sod roofs!" he shouted.

"He's right." Parks turned to Free, "Otherwise, Quanah would have burned us out this morning."

"I know we're all dragged out," Free said as the hunters collected near him and Parks. "But we need to get these men a proper burial before our friends return."

"Hey!" Henry Lease cried out from the alley beside Myers and Leonard's store. "Over here! It's Billy Tyler! They've killed him!"

"Is there anyone else we're missing?" Free quickly surveyed the group.

Billy Dixon took a quick head count. "That's seems to be all, Free."

"Then let's get to digging before Quanah decides he wants to fight some more."

By nightfall, Ike, Jacob, and Billy were laid to rest in a common grave north of The Walls. The distasteful job of removing the dead horses and oxen came next.

Parks stood over a number of horses close to the saloon. "This is going to take some doing. How are we going to move these animals?"

Free gazed over their dilemma. "I don't know, but if we can't figure something out it is going to get miserable inside that saloon."

"We'll use an old buffalo hunter's trick," Bat Masterson offered. "Bermuda, bring me some of those skins from the hide yard." The young skinner looked over at Free and Parks and winked to both men. "We'll tie some ropes to each corner of the hides and toss the animals on them. If enough of us pitch in we'll be able to skid them far enough away so the stench is tolerable," he grinned.

"Pull 'em or smell 'em," Bermuda laughed.

* * *

Later, after the streets were cleared, the exhausted men took their first rest of the day.

"I hope our friends at Camp Supply might learn what is going on here," Billy Dixon said as he stared into the approaching evening.

"I'm sure they will, Billy," Free offered. "It's just going to take awhile."

"What about these Indians?" Bermuda Carlisle stood in the prairie grass and kicked at one of the Cheyenne warriors.

Free ran a dried tongue over his parched lips. "If we don't bury them, we'll smell them for however long we stay trapped here."

"To blazes with burying these savages!" Bermuda replied and pulled a long bladed knife from his boot.

"Wait!" Free shouted angrily, "Let his soul be! Leave his hair, Bermuda!"

The hide hunter dropped to a knee and laughed. "I'm not taking his hair." He placed the knife against the slain warrior's throat. "I'll be taking his whole head!"

Chapter Fourteen

Adobe Walls, Texas, June 1874

In the approaching darkness, Quanah leaned on a dead cottonwood log and stared into the grim faces of the older chiefs. He pressed a poultice of grass and alder bark against his wound to stem his blood loss. A gathering of Comanche, Kiowa, and Cheyenne stood in silence around the council of chiefs still gathered at the fire pit. Esa-tai sat in the middle of the older chiefs, flanked by Lone Wolf, Stone Calf, He-Bear, Tabananaka, and Minimic.

The white-haired chief held the sacred pipe to his lips and drew deeply on the wooden tube. He passed the pipe to his left and exhaled the smoke. "Who among you shot Quanah's horse by accident?"

The crowd of warriors stayed quiet.

"We must know," the older chief continued, "for if it was not us, maybe these white men have the gift of a new gun that is strong medicine."

"No!" Esa-tai shouted and took to his feet. He pointed at the assembled Cheyenne. "The Cheyenne have broken the *puha* of the medicine paint by killing a skunk on the way to battle!"

A great murmur arose among all of those present and a Cheyenne warrior stepped forward.

"Esa-tai's medicine is weak!" he spoke rapidly

to the group. "The white hunters were not asleep as he said."

"Haaiiee!" Esa-tai screamed at his detractor. "The hide hunters were asleep! We have two scalps to prove it so!"

The Cheyenne brave did not back down from the Comanche medicine man, "It is as Maman-ti foretold; the Great Spirit did not show pity on us for this fight!"

The collected warriors nodded their heads in agreement and soon the soft murmur of whispers filled the air.

"Are the Cheyenne now afraid of the few hunters at Adobe Walls?" Esa-tai stared hard at the Cheyenne and folded his arms across his chest. "Talk to your own and ask who killed the skunk forbidden by the Great Spirit!"

The Cheyenne brave thumped his chest with his right hand. "The Cheyenne have fought many fights and killed many white men. We are not afraid to fight men, but we cannot fight strong magic. The hide hunters have shot Quanah and killed his pony! What say you about that, Wolf Prophet?"

Esa-tai pointed his right index finger at the massed warriors. "These white men do not have medicine. The Great Spirit only wanted to show the People that he does not side with us if we show disrespect. A skunk *was* killed by the Cheyenne! And the Cheyenne must make prayers to the Great Spirit asking for forgiveness!"

From the back of the congregation, a stocky Cheyenne brave named Hippy pushed his way through the gathered throng and approached the council. He lightly swatted his shoulder with a leather quirt at each step. "How does the Wolf Prophet answer for the fifteen warriors left dead on the battlefield?" Hippy asked and whipped the quirt harder. "And now our scouts say more hide hunters make their way to the Adobe Walls!" The rough leather left red welts with each swat. "While our brothers lie there, Wolf Prophet!" He jumped at Esa-tai with the quirt raised to strike. "Why don't you ride down in your magic paint and retrieve their bodies before the whites defile them?" He whipped the leather strap at Esa-tai's face. "What say you, Wolf Prophet?" he shouted sarcastically.

"Wait!" The old chief looked at the Cheyenne and spoke in a whisper. "We show weakness by fighting among ourselves."

Quanah pushed himself upright and dropped the poultice. "Listen to the old chief's wisdom. We still hold our medicine! Tonight we ride down to gather our dead. Tomorrow we ride down to kill all the intruders on our lands!"

As the June sun raced to join the morning sky, several bands of Kiowa, twenty-five abreast, marched their ponies back to the battleground. Lone Wolf circled his warriors from the southwest and hoped to surprise the hunters from the back of the stockaded hide yard.

Seven hundred yards from the buildings, a gruesome sight greeted his advancing war party. Fifteen wooden poles reflected conspicuously in the morning sun. The pickets were spaced an arm's length apart and planted straightaway from the hunter's wagons.

Lone Wolf stopped his band of warriors and

reached for the long glass. *"Pééy!"* He shouted in anger as he focused the glass on each pole. *"Pééy!"*

Little Boy leaned over his mustang's head and squinted at the poles, trying to detect the cause of Lone Wolf's anguish.

Lone Wolf glanced back at his group and poked the long glass into Little Boy's chest. "They have disfigured our dead," he whispered.

Little Boy settled the glass tube on the stakes and saw the heads of fifteen warriors atop the sharpened pickets. The same warriors whose bodies had laid too close to the hunters' buildings to retrieve last night. "Aaaiiihhheee!" he screamed.

Lone Wolf looked skyward and began a mournful chant in a coyote like tone. Soon the band of Kiowa behind him understood what the stakes represented and the warriors all followed in high-pitched wails. Lone Wolf howled for several minutes and when his grief was satiated, he turned his pony back east and walked the horse through the band of warriors.

"The Great Spirit is not with the Kiowa for this fight," he remarked in passing to each Kiowa brave. "It is best we go back to Elk Creek and join Maman-ti and the sun dancers."

Quanah watched the Kiowa depart Skunk Ridge in a slow procession. He knew many of the Cheyenne and Comanche would follow Lone Wolf's decision. Esa-tai's medicine was now known to all of the bands as ineffective and weak against the hide hunters. He rose and setting aside the pain of his bullet wound, strode confidently over to his horse and jumped on the steed's back.

The older white haired chief looked up from

the council circle and blew smoke from his pipe. "Where are you going, Quanah?"

"I want to ride there," he pointed, "to the flat top mountain. I want to observe the source of the hide hunter's medicine."

"Take Esa-tai with you." The older chief drew upon his pipe, "and let him observe as well."

Quanah nodded and looked over to Esa-tai who sat atop his horse staring with an open mouth at the departing Kiowa.

"Hey Comanche medicine man," one of the Kiowa braves called out, "maybe you are the pole cat the Cheyenne should have eaten."

The rest of the Kiowa laughed loudly at the remark and passed the joke down the line to each brave.

On the small butte east of the Adobe Walls Creek, Quanah sat with a delegation of twenty warriors. He pointed to a stand of plum trees south of the hide hunters' buildings.

"If we keep inside the cover of the plum thicket and stay west in the high grasses we can avoid the long rifles and kill the hunters as they come to their well for water."

Stone Calf sat next to the Comanche leader and nodded his approval. "They have no horses to ride away and they must have water soon."

Quanah continued, knowing he might salvage the raid if they could kill the hunters. "And if we keep others from riding to their aid, we can still win this siege."

The other warriors murmured in excitement at Quanah's confidence.

"What about him?" Stone Calf pointed to a distant Esatai.

"He has suffered humiliation enough for one hundred warriors." Quanah glanced quickly at the Wolf Prophet, "His medicine is gone."

"And what of you, Quanah?" Stone Calf asked.

Quanah leaned toward his warrior friend, "I am a warrior. No matter what happens here, there will always be another day to fight."

The distinct but faint sound of a long rifle echoed from the buildings.

Quanah threw a searching gaze toward the last building in the settlement line. A wispy puff of smoke issued from a small slot in the adobe wall. He looked back at the assembled group, and laughed, "Look! The hunters think they can hit us from so far away!"

Before he finished, a warrior on the far right of the group slumped and fell from his horse. Instinctively, the remaining warriors turned their ponies and rushed for safety below the crest of the butte. The startled braves stared in amazement toward Adobe Walls and then watched helplessly as the downed warrior writhed on the ground.

"The medicine guns can shoot for a mile and kill The People."

Quanah listened to the whispers from the warriors around him and heard the fear in their voices. Even in the oppressive morning heat, a passing breeze chilled his back and a dream clouded his vision. He turned and looked at his fellow brothers, but all of his friends were gone. He stood alone on the butte and stared at a building cloud of dust on the eastern horizon.

Buffalo, he smiled. He shaded his eyes to watch the lifeline of the People returning to the Kwahada. His heart felt happy and he offered a silent prayer to the Great Spirit.

Above, a small cloud appeared under the sun and a spreading shade moved quickly across his back. He stared at the sky and laughed. "This is a good day!" he declared. He tossed his gaze back to the buffalo and opened his arms wide to the warmth of the sun.

However the sun turned cold, and his smile turned to sadness. For out of the giant dust cloud an endless line of covered wagons now appeared and rolled west.

Chapter Fifteen

Adobe Walls, Texas, June 1874

Free had watched many spectacular displays of marksmanship in his life, but none could match the shot Billy Dixon threw up at the Indian sitting horseback on the butte overlooking Adobe Walls.

Parks looked through the rifle port and watched the startled Indians scramble for safety. "That shot will do more for our cause than anything else we could have attempted this morning."

Free jerked opened the oak door and stepped into the morning sun. He glanced south to Rath's and shouted, "Billy Dixon! Now that was some shot!"

Parks followed Free outside, grinned and said, "Amen to that!"

Billy Dixon exited Rath's store and squinted in the bright sunlight. The other hide hunters strolled behind him and patted his back in appreciation.

"How'd you know it was me made the shot?" Billy surveyed the surrounding landscape and greeted Free with a boyish smirk.

"I reckoned no other man in Rath's would waste two bits worth of ammunition to attempt such a shot."

"That's a fair assessment for sure," Billy said and began to laugh.

Parks looked west, searching for any sign of

Horse and issued a series of loud whistles. "Horse!" he hollered. "Com'on Horse!"

"You really think he survived the Comanche?" Billy asked.

Free met Billy in the street, midway between Hanrahan's and Rath's. "You'd be surprised about that pony. He's as sneaky as a government politician."

Parks stared west and whistled again, "Com'on now, Horse!" He looked over at Billy and shook the buffalo hunter's hand. "Your shot will have that war council rethinking Quanah's wisdom of a war party."

"I sure hope so." Billy looked toward the butte. "How far you think that is?"

"Three quarters of a mile at least." Free said, "A long way in anyone's book."

"It's about time." Parks observed a cloud of dust kicked up on the western horizon.

"Well I'll be darn!" Billy removed his hat and scratched his head.

"What did I tell you?" Free said, amused. Suddenly the day seemed brighter and he knew their chances of making it out of The Walls alive were dramatically better than just an hour earlier.

Parks stepped forward and focused on the fast approaching cloud. "Now that's a well trained pony." He shaded his eyes, "Even if I do say so."

Horse slowed to a trot as he approached the backside of Rath's store. He maneuvered through the alley and walked with a swagger up to Parks.

"Horse!" Parks turned his head sideways and looked at the animal. "Where you been for so long?"

Horse nodded his head rapidly as if to scold

Parks. He whinnied, showed his teeth and bumped his owner playfully with his nose.

Parks rubbed the mustang's ears and grinned. "Good boy, Horse. Good boy."

"So what do you think these Indians will offer now?" Bat Masterson asked as he walked toward the assembled group of men.

Parks turned back to the east and reached for his tobacco pouch. "More than likely, they will stay in the high grass and not offer a target for your Sharps. I think they understand the message Billy delivered to them this morning."

"The farther away the better," Bat said and surveyed the hills behind The Walls.

"It will definitely hold in our favor if they do keep their distance," Free said, relieved. "I'm still beat as to how that door in Hanrahan's stayed put."

"I think there's one little flaw in your theory, Parks," Billy grimaced.

"What are you talking about?" Parks looked over at the hunter, concerned.

"Well, If I'm not mistaken" Billy pointed to the southeast. "That appears to be a Comanche brave riding to beat the devil toward us."

Chapter Sixteen

Adobe Walls, Texas, June 1874

T he lone Comanche brave approached Adobe Walls in a courageous display of power and primitive savagery. The brightly painted warrior both frightened and enthralled the hide hunters watching from the street.

"Everybody, hold your weapons." Free stepped forward. "What do you figure he's doing, Parks?" he asked calmly.

"Riding in alone, I figure he's game to fight or wants to palaver a bit."

"Well he's got grit, that's for sure." Billy Dixon stared suspiciously at the Comanche.

"He will gain a great coup riding in here unannounced and alone," Parks offered in respect.

The warrior stopped a hundred yards from Rath's and paraded his pony in an easterly direction for several paces. In perfect harmony with his mustang's gait, he swung his shield high across his face and then lowered it to his side. A circle of eagle feathers decorated the finely tanned shield and a series of black stripes covered half of the armament. The brave's face glistened with blackened grease that streaked horizontally across his eyes and forehead. Turning his pony back west, he trotted the animal like royalty and shouted to the assembled hunters, "Which of you is brave enough to fight me like a warrior?"

"Appears to be makin' a challenge," Bat Masterson declared.

"Killing so far away is not an honor!" the brave shouted. "Face to face! That is the way a warrior fights his enemies!

Free became quiet and sized up the Comanche warrior.

"What's running through your head?" Parks asked.

"I figure I'll need his horse if I aim to make it home anytime soon."

Parks looked startled. "You're not really considering fighting him, are you?"

Free shrugged. "I rather fight him afoot than on horseback. The Comanche are heap more frightening mounted than on the ground."

"Is there not a warrior among the hide hunters?" The brave stabbed his lance into the ground. "Not one of you has the courage to answer the challenge from The People's warrior, To'sa-woonit?"

Free stepped forward and dropped his gun belt. "Step off your horse, To'sa-woonit, and I'll honor your request!"

To'sa-woonit hopped from his pony with little effort. He dropped the reins and allowed the animal to graze unstaked. Unlike most Comanche warriors, he was tall, close to six feet in height and dressed in breechcloth, moccasins, and leggings. "I have taken many scalps but never from a buffalo man." He motioned for Free to join him at a distance from the others.

Free stepped purposefully toward To'sa-woonit in long graceful strides. "How do you wish to proceed?"

With a startling shriek, the Comanche rushed Free brandishing a war axe.

"AAAiiihheee!" He sprinted forward, slapping the stone head of the weapon on the top of Free's shoulder, spoke softly into his ear, then charged on.

Free felt lightning spread across his back and his stomach heaved. Before he could think, he dropped to one knee and grabbed for his shoulder. Slender white flashes danced across his eyes.

To'sa-woonit stopped, tilted his head and smirked at the hide hunters before turning back to Free. "The buffalo man goes down easy," he called out.

Free struggled to his feet and realized he had no sensation in his right arm. Steadied, he backed up and circled to his right, trying to keep his left arm close to the brave. "I'll do better next go 'round," he offered.

To'sa-woonit raised the war axe and rushed forward with the quickness of a big cat. "*Haa!*" he shouted.

Free crouched slightly and waited. As To'sa-woonit prepared to strike, Free dropped to the ground, swept his right leg across the back of the Comanche's left ankle and upended him in a flailing of arms and legs.

Unprepared for this tactic, To'sa-woonit hit the ground with a deafening thud. As his head slammed against the hardened summer earth, the stone axe bounced from his hand and landed several feet away.

Free regained his feet quickly and stood over the downed warrior. He rubbed his shoulder in a kneading motion hoping to return some feeling to his arm. "Get up!" he screamed.

To'sa-woonit threw open his eyes, rubbed the back of his head and searched for his axe.

"It's over there!" Free pointed to the weapon. "Is To'sa-woonit afraid to fight like a warrior or does he need his axe for bravery?" he taunted.

To'sa-woonit screamed in anger and jumped to his feet. His eyes blackened with the hate of a caged animal. He lowered his shoulder and rushed Free once more.

Free knew if he stood still, To'sa-woonit's force would drive him to the ground. Without hesitation, he screamed and raced headlong for the Comanche. As the two collided, Free grabbed To'sa-woonit around the neck and tried to wrestle him down.

Better prepared now, To'sa-woonit lifted his shoulder hard into Free's chest and flipped him helplessly to the prairie floor.

Free felt the breath rush from his lungs and a burning pain spread across his chest. He gained his feet and circled warily around the Comanche desperately gasping for air.

To'sa-woonit snarled and pulled a long-bladed knife from his waist. He waved the blade back and forth to show the sharpened edge and let a wide grin come across his mouth. "I will take your scalp, buffalo man and hang it with pride from my pony's mane!"

Free moved in closer and watched the knife's movements. He knew the Comanche would slice him with small strikes so the pain and blood would last longer. His right arm began to ache, a signal the feeling would return soon. He feigned right with his upper body and then swept his right leg against the back of To'sa-woonit's left knee.

Once more, the Comanche warrior hit the ground in a heap. Anger seethed from eyes.

"AAAiiihheee!" To'sa-woonit howled and sprang to his feet.

Free knew the warrior's fury would work to his advantage. He circled the Comanche once more and waited patiently. To'sa-woonit set on him again with the knife raised high above his head. Free ducked and feinted right again. To'sa-woonit, expecting the leg whip, hopped to his left and glanced at Free's right leg.

Seeing To'sa-woonit's head glancing downward, Free swung his left arm in a wide arc and hit the Comanche with a powerful fist to the nose. To'sa-woonit went limp and fell straightaway to the ground. With blood gushing, he lay still and stared blankly at the sky.

Free stood over the brave for several seconds to make sure his foe wasn't feigning. When To'sa-woonit didn't move, Free rubbed his shoulder and walked toward the Comanche pony. "Easy," he whispered to the horse and reached carefully for the lead rein, "you and I are going to become friends."

Parks and the rest of the Adobe Walls inhabitants rushed toward Free. "Are you OK?" Parks grabbed for his exhausted friend.

"I reckon I've felt better."

Billy Dixon reached for the Comanche horse's reins and offered a shoulder to Free. "That was some exhibition."

Free glanced back at the still lifeless Comanche. "I was lucky."

Bermuda Carlisle walked rapidly toward Free

and frowned. "Why didn't you kill him when you had the chance?" He charged by, reaching for his knife as he went.

"I didn't kill him on account, Bermuda, and neither will you!" Free turned from the helping hands of Parks and Billy and grabbed the unpredictable hide hunter by the collar.

Bermuda slapped Free's hand away and gripped the handle of his Colt. "On account of what, Indian lover?" he shouted, provoked to act.

"On account, *that* Comanche is a white man! That's what!"

Chapter Seventeen

Adobe Walls, Texas, June 1874

The group sidestepped as Free turned to face Bermuda. "Leave it be, Bermuda," he said icily. The hide hunter tightened his grip on the Colt and then thinking the better of it removed his hand. "Aw, to blazes with you, Indian lover."

"Are you sure?" Parks moved between Free and Bermuda and glanced at the prone figure lying in the tall grass.

"I'm sure." Free kept a watchful eye on Bermuda.

"How? How are you sure?" Billy Dixon let his jaw go slack and shook his head.

"Yeah, Cowboy. How?" Bermuda looked around Parks.

Free stared hard into the faces of the hunters who now formed a circle around him. "Blue eyes," he said, "He had blue eyes."

"Wha? What kinda nonsense are you speaking?" Bermuda said and stood openmouthed.

Parks moved within inches of Free's face and spoke deliberately. "You're sure?"

"I was as close to him as you and I right now. He may be living with the Comanche, but he's a white man."

Parks looked back to where the brave lay. "Appears he's left us." He searched quickly around the prairie and issued a low whistle.

"What?" Free turned, incredulously.

"Your white Comanche is up and gone." Parks looked carefully for the movement of any grass stalks.

"No white man moves like that." Billy Dixon scanned the prairie. "I've always heard a Comanche could untie a staked horse in a crowd of white men and never be noticed."

"Snake people." Parks placed his hand around his Colt handle, "that's what the other tribes call them."

"Blazes!" Bermuda cursed, "I knew better than to let him go."

"Let's all keep our senses and move back to Hanrahan's." Parks continued to search the prairie beyond them.

"I can't." Free grabbed for the Comanche pony's reins. "I need to head out now."

"You can't leave with this horse." Billy seized Free's wrist. "We need to send more riders out for help and that horse offers us another chance."

"Take your hand away, Billy." Free tightened his jaw and narrowed his eyes. "If you need a horse get one the same as I did!"

"Have you gone loco?" Billy turned to Parks for help. "What's got into him?"

"What is it, Free?" Parks moved between the two men.

"It's something To'sa-woonit said out there."

"What? What could he have said to get you so riled?" Billy Dixon backed up two steps.

Free slipped the lead rein over the mustang's ears and swung up on the pony. "He said a medicine man called Maman-ti was sending a band of Kiowa for my family."

Chapter Eighteen

Anderson Farm, Texas, July 1874

A sweltering heat simmered in the morning air and boiled over onto the Texas landscape. Unseen moisture dampened skin and cloth alike, smothering all that drew breath under its soggy weight. Clara Anderson labored in what little shade the west side of her home afforded. She looked skyward and prayed silently for a gentle wind, *God's little gift*, her mother called a cooling breeze.

The day was remarkably still for West Texas, and a dark foreboding twisted in her thoughts, keeping her disturbed as to the reason. She worked diligently with needle and thread to mend one of Free's shirts in the hope that the work would keep the uneasiness at bay.

The years following the war had been good to Clara. Born an Alabama slave, her realized dreams of marrying a man of her own choosing, giving birth to free children, and living as a freed woman, once seemed an unreachable blessing reserved only for other people.

Alone and absorbed in her sewing, Clara felt a small breeze meander through the shade, bringing an immediate, if only brief, relief from the heat. *Thank you, Mother.* She smiled and then allowed her thoughts to wander back to her first master, Mr. Browning.

As a slave child, she found him to be a tolerable owner. As a woman, she knew him to be an insufferable mean man. She recalled one particular morning in the Browning kitchen. After cleaning the dishes, Mrs. Browning offered her a slice of fresh baked cake. She had never seen cake before and the sweet smell that drifted through the kitchen that morning was as fragrant as honeysuckle. She had stared at the cake sitting on its white plate for the longest time, afraid to spoil its simple beauty with a fork.

And while she hesitated, Mr. Browning entered the kitchen. "What's this?" He looked at Mrs. Browning and lifted the cake from the table.

"Get out, Clara!" he ordered, "You know better than to sit at the table!"

She fled from the kitchen that morning thinking she had done wrong, and even today, she could still hear Mr. Browning's harangue, "Don't be bringing cake out to the slaves, Anna! They'll just get a likin' for it and its unlikely they'll ever get to taste it again!

Now, so many years later living without the obligations of slavery, she came to make sense of Mr. Browning's words. Just like cake, once a person tasted freedom, the more freedom that person wanted. Untroubled freedom.

She came to appreciate the small freedoms gained, but the toilsome effort of protecting those freedoms greeted her each day like the rising sun. And with Free gone for so much of the time to earn money, she had become both the sole parent and protector for their son and their home. It was a responsibility she loved, but it was unceasing and relentless. A small tear formed at the corner of her eyes and the pangs of loneliness clinched her tightly. *Quit your complaining, Clara Anderson,* she scolded, *and be happy for the things that most folks take for granted.*

Five year old William Parks and Dog raced from the corner of the house toward the mustang corral scattering guinea hens along the way. Oblivious to the morning heat, William Parks jumped on the second rail of the corral and peered between the bars at the horses inside.

"Heyahh!" he swung an imaginary rope at the ponies. "Gitayup now!" he mimicked his father's calls.

Dog, a gift from the Kiowa in 1868, had saved Free's life twice that year and was William Parks' best friend.

"William Parks Anderson!" Clara dabbed her eyes and called from her perch, "You be careful over there and *do not* nettle those horses!" She ducked her head and smiled, *So much like his father.*

Free and Parks had left two weeks earlier to deliver horses to Camp Supply and although their journeys often kept them away from home much longer something felt wrong this morning. *Quit worrying so, Clara.* She pursed her lips and tried to concentrate on her sewing. But she could not stop her mind from churning in concern. Unknown to Free, she carried their second child and lately she seemed to be all emotions.

She finished a series of stitches and then let her gaze wander to the corral, but William Parks had already moved on and was not in sight. "William Parks!" she called out, "You get back where I can see you, young man!"

* * *

William Parks dragged a willow branch in the dirt on the far side of the mustang corral. He watched in great concentration at the squiggly line that trailed his every step. Dog followed at his heels and tried to make the boy play with him by snapping at the stick. William Parks laughed at Dog's antics and held the branch teasingly underneath the dog's nose.

Dog clamped his powerful jaws on the branch and held it securely. He growled playfully at the boy and urged him to play tug. William Parks grabbed one end of the stick, shook it back and forth, and then let go. Dog growled, shook the branch rapidly from side to side, and dropped to his belly, contented to chew on the bark.

William Parks laughed, reached down and grabbed the stick again. Dog growled in mock anger, jumped to his feet and turned his head away from the boy. William Parks held on with a firm handhold and proceeded to shake the stick from side to side once more all the while howling in laughter.

Clara heard her son's contagious laugh and let a wide grin cross her face. "What's so funny, William Parks?" she laughed aloud.

The five year old lifted his head at his mother's voice and held a finger to his lips. "Shush," he whispered and then yanked the branch from the unsuspecting dog's mouth.

He held the stick as high as he could into the air and turned in a small circle on his tiptoes, trying to keep it away from Dog. Dog jumped at the extended hand and tried to reclaim the branch. Unable to latch onto the stick, he crashed against

William Parks' chest and knocked the boy to the ground.

William Parks landed in a heap and lay his head in the dirt. He laughed hysterically and called out, "Bad Dog!" He shook his finger in mock anger, "Bad, bad Dog!" he frowned.

Dog sat back on his haunches and stared at the boy with his head turned sideways. William Parks pushed himself to a sitting position and held the branch toward Dog.

Dog straightened his head and looked past the stick. He opened his mouth and bared his teeth in a frightening display. A low guttural growl rumbled in his chest.

William Parks became quiet as a shadow darkened the ground in front of him. Thinking a cloud covered the sun, he looked up only to see a clear sky.

Dog rose from his haunches and exposed his canines in a primitive warning of *stay away.* "What is it, Dog?" William Parks turned to see what stood behind him. Blinded by the morning sun, he could only make out the outline of a crouched solitary figure.

"Bang! Bang!" he pointed the stick at the silhouette.

The shadowy impression, dressed in a long shirt belted with silver, leaned over so he was face to face with William Parks. The man had flowing black hair braided on one side with a beaded eagle feather. His face was sun worn and appeared leather-like. A series of black concentric circles covered one side of his bare chest.

Dog started toward the man. Saliva dripped

from the corners of his mouth and the hair on his back stood stiffly at attention.

The man shot a quick glance at Dog and bared his teeth. He pointed a finger at the animal and issued a firm whoosh. Dog stopped, unsure as what to do and then quieted. The man looked toward a stand of cedar a hundred yards to the south and waved an arm back and forth across his head. Turning back to William Parks, he asked gruffly, "Where is your father, boy?"

Clara stood straight-backed and stern faced at the Tonkawa and twenty soldiers in front of her. She motioned for William Parks to take a position behind her. The boy stared up at the Tonkawa who held his hand firmly. The Tonkawa released his hand and William Parks raced for his mother without hesitation and hid behind the safety of her dress.

"Who do you think you are?" She shouted angrily at the Tonkawa. Her initial shock had now changed to anger. "You do not ride on my land and take hold of my child!" she stomped the ground to emphasize her point. "And you," she pointed to the mounted soldiers behind the Tonkawa, "You should know better than this!"

The Tonkawa took a step forward, "I am Job." He proclaimed proudly, "A friend." He patted his chest several times.

"I know who you are!" Clara replied. She was familiar with the Tonkawa. Their camps were nearby and many of the braves worked as military scouts for the regiments at Fort Griffin. "What do you want here?"

William Parks peered around his mother's skirt and watched the soldier's wince at his mother's anger.

"Ma'am, We've come here . . ."

"Don't you Ma'am, me, soldier!" Clara interrupted, "just tell me what you want!"

A young soldier, no more than eighteen, straightened and said, "We're here to see your husband."

Clara relaxed slightly, but kept the edge in her voice. "About what?"

"Colonel Mackenzie would like a sit down with him, Ma'am."

"What did I tell you about Ma'am'ing me!" Clara scolded once more.

"Sorry, Ma' . . . Mrs. Anderson." The clearly uncomfortable soldier corrected himself. "Would Mr. Anderson be home?"

"He'll be returning shortly. I'll make sure he receives the message."

"Thank you, Ma' . . . Mrs. Anderson." The soldier tapped the brim of his hat. "I guess we'll be taking our leave then."

Clara watched the soldiers turn their horses back toward Fort Griffin. "Where does your colonel want to meet with my husband?" she called out.

"We'll be heading back to Fort Concho today, but the colonel will be back in the area by month's end," the young soldier replied.

Job grinned, "The little Anderson is a brave son."

"Go on!" Clara motioned for the man to leave.

The Tonkawa chief re-mounted and rode out slowly with the detail of soldiers.

As the group departed, Dog strolled over to Clara and stood by her side.

"And you!" she glared at the dog and scolded him with a shaking finger. "Where were you while this was all going on? You better start doing your job!"

Dog arched his back high in the air, lowered his head and moved off with his tail between his legs.

"Goodness." Clara pulled William Parks from behind her skirt and held him tightly. "Don't ever scare your mother like that again," she whispered then kissed the top of his head.

William Parks kissed his mother's cheek and pointed at Dog. "Bad dog!" he mimicked his mother's voice laughingly.

Big Bow and three Kiowa braves sat on a small rise above the clear fork of the Brazos. He watched the Tonkawa and horse soldiers converse with the buffalo man's woman.

"So the buffalo woman has the protection of the *Ta-'ka-i*." He loosened the rein and turned his pony's head northward. "There is nothing more to be done here," he said impassively. "Let's ride back and join the Owl Prophet in his sun dance. After that, maybe the Kiowa can finally soak the land in *Teñá-nego* blood."

Chapter Nineteen

Palo Duro Canyon, Texas, July 1874

Under a forbidding green sky, Free raced To'sa-woonit's pony through the juniper stands and across the red and yellow-layered cliffs of the Palo Duro canyon. Parks rode fifty yards back and kept a watchful eye on their trail and the building storm.

Free had figured the quickest and safest way home was to skirt the bands of Comanche, Kiowa, and Cheyenne raiding parties spread around Adobe Walls and the surrounding buffalo grounds. He had avoided a possible confrontation with Billy Dixon earlier in the day when a large group of buffalo hunters straggled into the Walls, most with horses.

A large raindrop splattered on Free's shoulder, and thunder rumbled across the sky. Free pulled rein on the Comanche pony and stopped near the canyon rim. He looked over the pony's shoulder to the distant floor below.

"What do you reckon that sky is going to do?" he asked as Parks rode up even with him.

Parks appraised the billowing clouds as a single raindrop hit Horse's neck. "Looks to be carrying lightning and hail."

"More fuss I suspect." Free scratched his head in frustration. "After fighting Indians for two days, you'd figure a man alone on a stretch of vacant openness might face the prospect of a little peace." He held his palm up to the slowly increasing rainfall. "But now it appears nature itself is itching for a fight."

Parks lowered his head and flashed a scant grin. "Probably not a good idea for us to be sitting exposed on this canyon rim."

Free nodded and searched for any sign of tracks leading into the canyon. A charge of lightning flashed in the west, and the early afternoon sky darkened. "If we can discover a trail, we might find an overhang to shelter in until the storm blows by." He moved the Indian pony slowly along the rim and searched intently for a way down. "Here!" he shouted, "looks like a deer trail!"

Parks shot a quick glance at the western horizon. Great sheets of rain pushed across the prairie and raced for them, accompanied by an unfriendly wind. He looked over to Free and then threw a quick glance down the deer trail. "That'll do," he said.

Both men dismounted and with urgent caution led their ponies down into the great canyon with a soaker on their heels.

A stream of muddy water rushed down the small deer trail swirling around the men's ankles and making each step a treacherous undertaking. The sudden and violent downburst fell with such menacing force that the path was becoming impossible to navigate.

"We've got to find some cover!" Parks screamed over the roar of the storm. "We best not go down to the floor! I reckon it's a river by now!"

A crack of lightning lit up the darkened sky and briefly exposed an outcropping of rock a short distance down the trail.

"Look!" Free hollered and pointed to the cleft of flat stone jutting from the wall of the canyon. "We're in luck!"

They inched their way down into the canyon with great care. Free held the reins tight in hand on the Comanche mustang and kept the horse's head close against his shoulder. Parks followed tentatively, leading Horse, he trudged in the gray muck blended under the hooves of To'sa-woonit's mustang.

The overhang extended five feet above the canyon and served as a canopy for a small entryway not visible from the trail. Free stared at the cave opening and turned back to Parks. "There's an opening here but it will be a tight squeeze getting the horses inside."

"Give it a try! If your pony can't get through we'll stake both of them outside. We don't have any other choice."

Free nodded and after a little coaxing disappeared through the opening pulling the pony behind him.

Inside, complete darkness faced the men. A gray shaft of light from the opening exposed enough of the natural enclosure to indicate they stood in a very large cave.

"Can you see the back wall?" Parks asked. He advanced forward furtively in the enveloping blackness.

"This blackness is thicker than a blanket," Free answered. "I can't see anything."

Parks tried to locate any obstacles in his path by holding his right hand away from his body and waving it back and forth. After several steps, his knee knocked against a solid object that sounded like wood. "Blazes!" he shouted and grabbed his leg.

"What is it?" Free turned back, "Are you OK?"

"He probably bumped against my gun crates." A voice filled the blackness. "There is a torch and matches on top of the crate, *señor*. Why don't you light it and turn toward me with great care. I have always thought it rude to kill a man before I've seen his face."

Chapter Twenty

La Cueva de Comanchero, Texas, July 1874

The noxious odor of rotten eggs accompanied a plume of black smoke toward the cave ceiling. The torch gradually danced into a yellow flame illuminating the surrounding blackness.

"*Gracias señors, gracias.*" The ghostly voice wandered across the cave. "*Buenos tardes.*"

"Who are you?" Free asked.

The figure lit a torch ensconced on the cave wall behind him, "I was here first, *señor*. Who are you?"

As the torch turned into flame, a short, slender figure grew out of the darkness. The man held a pearl handle Colt in each hand.

"I'm Free Anderson, and this is my partner, Parks Scott."

"Well, Free Anderson, have your partner, Parks Scott, place his torch in the crevice behind him."

Parks did as he was ordered and then turned, studying the man carefully. "Comanchero?" he asked.

"So many questions *señor*. The both of you, raise your right hands and slowly unbuckle those gun belts with your left hands. Slowly, *por favor.*"

"We only stopped here to get out of the storm," Free explained.

"Shhh. Now walk over there." The man motioned toward the back wall. "Face the wall with your hands up and keep very quiet."

Free and Parks obliged the man and moved away from the horses. Against the wall, Parks wheeled and stared at the figure. "You're trading guns to the Comanche," he stated.

The man smiled at Parks while he grasped the willow hoop woven into the Comanche pony's mane. "I know of this horse. How did you gringos come by him?"

"A friend let me borrow him," Free replied.

"A friend?"

"Yes, a friend."

"How long you know this friend, *señor*?" The man picked up the discarded gun belts.

"Long enough to borrow his horse."

"And this friend, he has a name?"

Free stared straight into his captor's eyes, "To'sa-woonit," he replied nonchalantly.

The man studied the Comanche pony once more and then sat on the rifle crate. He chewed on his lower lip, deep in thought. "I know this Comanche, To'sa-woonit, *señor*. I have never known him to be so kind."

"Well, he was kind enough to warn me of a raid upon my family." Free shrugged, "My horse was stolen, so he allowed me to borrow his."

"I don't know, *señor*. It still does not sound like the Comanche I know."

"If you know him and if you do trade guns with the Comanche, then you also know To'sa-woonit would not like his friends treated so."

The man looked out the cave entrance and exhaled a deep breath. "Maybeso, maybenot. This I know, two men show up at my hiding place for rifles. Rifles that I trade to the Indians. This has not happened in my eight years of being a trader. You, *señor,* tell me it is just a coincidence. Maybeso, but maybenot. I am, how you say, between the fence and the mustang."

"We're just trying to get back home. That's all," Free said coolly.

The man frowned, "And where is this home, *señor?*"

"On the old Comanche reservation. My wife and son are there."

"It is not wise for a man to leave his woman in such a hard land, *señor.* No?"

"Lucky, we are friends to both the Comanche and the Kiowa," Free stated matter-of-factly.

The man nodded slowly. "The storm has moved on. Maybe you two should do the same."

Free and Parks rotated from the wall, relieved.

"Much obliged," Free exhaled quietly.

The man hung the gun belts around Horse's saddle and then moved back to the south wall. He motioned with his Colt for Free and Parks to leave. *"Vaya con dios, señors.* And if by chance you accidentally seek shelter here again, know that I will kill you both."

Free nodded his gratitude and followed Parks, stopping before he exited. "I didn't catch your name, mister."

"Tafoya. Jose Piedad Tafoya."

Chapter Twenty-one

Clear Fork Country, Texas, July 1874

Northwest of the Anderson homestead, a covey of quail broke the late afternoon silence in a sudden rush of flight. Startled by the noisy thrashing, Dog sprang to his feet and thrust his nose high into the air. He sniffed rapidly in several directions all the while growling in a low, continuous rumble. Agitated by the birds and vexed by his inability to detect a strange scent, he grumbled once more and lay back down with an uneasiness that kept his ears at attention.

Clara heard the prolonged growl and looked out the kitchen door. She gazed past the roused dog into the distance as the spooked quail jumped again. She pushed at the screen door and stepped outside. "What is it, Dog?"

Dog shared Clara's apprehension, he stood and raised the hair on his back. He paced on the porch, disturbed by the unseen intruder and pulled his mouth taut exposing his canines. Out on the prairie, the quail spooked once more and flew from the ground. Dog stuck his nose into the air and honed in on a scent that rode on the wind from the northwest. He growled deeply and with an explosive charge sprinted into the open prairie with a loud series of barks that warned any stranger to stay away.

Clara shaded her eyes and looked toward the

horizon. A cold shiver tingled along her spine, a reminder of the danger that might be lurking close by. Dog had stopped forty yards out, and his incessant yipping served only to increase her fear. He alternated between sitting and standing, but his vocalization was unvarying and continuous.

Suddenly, he became quiet. As if on command, Dog sat and wagged his tail from side to side. He started forward several times only to stop and sit back down. In each instance a high-pitched whine issued from his throat.

Clara studied Dog's posture with a careful eye and then scanned the horizon for any movement. After several seconds of deliberation, she walked back to the open kitchen door and called inside, "William Parks Anderson. Hurry outside. Your father has come home."

Clara brushed William Park's shirt and holding the boy's hand walked at a quick pace to the edge of the prairie. She ran her free hand down her shirt and onto the front of her denim pants trying to press the wrinkles from the garments.

William Parks held his mother's hand and searched the flat land before him for any sign of his father. With his free hand, he petted Dog in long sweeping strokes and questioned, "Where's Daddy?" Dog sensed the boy's excitement and wagged his tail rapidly while sniffing at the air.

Within minutes, two shadowy figures dotted the horizon, running toward them atop the unmistakable gait of mustangs. Clara touched her chest and squeezed gently on William Park's hand.

William Parks, unable to contain his energy any longer, wrested his hand from his mother's grip and raced for the pair shouting, "Home! You're home!" Dog bolted with the boy and raced beside him, barking with each shout.

Free dismounted in one quick motion and picked up his son. He swung the boy into his arms and beamed broadly. "William Parks! Your daddy's come home!" Dog ran circles around the two and with an open mouth begged for attention.

Free held the boy at arm's length and kissed his cheek. "William Parks! Look at you! You've grown a foot since I've been gone!"

"Dog was bad." The boy offered. "Bad dog!"

"Dog was bad?" Free laughed.

William Parks nodded his head as response.

"Free!" Clara approached on a run.

Free lowered William Parks to the ground and raced toward her. "Clara!" he drew her into his chest and held her tightly, "Am I glad to see you!"

Clara smiled and held her head tight against Free. "Welcome home," she whispered. "It seems like you've been gone forever."

"Are you and William Parks OK?" he asked in a quiet voice.

"No questions now." She stared into his eyes, "Kiss me."

William Parks bent slightly at the waist and laughed loudly, "Mommy and daddy are kissing."

Free and Clara both laughed at the boy's declaration and broke away from their embrace. Free tickled the boy's stomach. "You think that's funny?"

The boy laughed, shook his head rapidly and then ran toward Parks.

Free turned back to Clara and gazed into her

eyes, "It's just that, we ran into some trouble with Indians along the way and one threatened that . . ."

"Shhh," Clara placed a finger against his lips. "There will be plenty of time for that talk later. Right now let's get you some food." She looked at Parks and smiled, "Welcome home."

Parks tipped his hat and dismounted. "Hello, Clara." He lifted William Parks into his arms and swung him around in a wide arc onto Horse's back. "Sorry, I kept your husband away so long."

"I have a suspicion it was not your doing, Parks. Come to the house with us and let me fix you men a decent meal."

"Thanks, Clara, but you two need some alone time." Parks reached for the Comanche mustang's reins, "I'll put up this pony, and then I'm heading to The Flats for a hot bath and shave."

"Where's Spirit?" Clara stared at the strange mustang.

Free placed his finger against her lips and whispered, "Shhh. Remember, let's get some food in me first."

Later, after William Parks was asleep, Free and Clara sat at the kitchen table and over coffee shared their experiences of the past two weeks.

Clara reached across the table and placed both her hands on top of Free's left hand, "What's going to happen to us?"

Free set his coffee down and stroked her hands with gentle affection. "I'm afraid the Kiowa and the Comanche are riled by the buffalo hunters and aim to shed blood." He slowly looked up and let his gaze rest on Clara. "Truth is, I think I've stepped into the middle of this fight because I tried to help one side take care of their dead." Free pulled his hands away and leaned back in his chair. "Parks warned me not to get involved."

"Helping those in need can't be avoided so easily. You know that, Free."

Free winced and thought back to the time, Clara had risked her life to help him. "I'm sorry, Clara. I'm sorry I've been gone for so much of the time, and I'm sorry I've got us all into this mess. It seems life keeps handing us one problem after another."

Clara frowned and clasped Free's hand, "You will not think like that, Free. You've never felt pity for yourself or for us since we met, and I will not let you start now."

Free leaned forward and intertwined both their hands together. "Well be warned then; I suspect this Col. Mackenzie is going to ask Parks and me to lead them to the Comanche and Kiowa camps."

Taken aback, Clara studied her husband's face and then asked, "And what will you tell him?"

Free shrugged,

"I don't know. If I say no, we'll be called Indian lovers and shunned by the military and all our neighbors. If I say yes, then the Kiowa will say I betrayed them and place a bounty on my head. I can't see that either answer benefits us."

"Can't you just say you don't want to be involved?"

Free exhaled a soft breath and dragged his hand across his mouth, "This country was born of fighting, and I reckon it can't grow up until it gets its fill of battle. And whether I like it or not, it requires men like Parks and me to get our hands bloodied on a regular occasion . . . And there's something else."

"What?" Clara leaned in close. "What else?"

"If we don't honor the army's request, you can bet the government will never buy another S&A mustang."

Clara lowered her head and softly kissed Free's hands. "Free."

"Yes, Clara."

"There's something I need to tell you."

"What?" Free squeezed Clara's hands.

Clara raised her head and gazed into Free's eyes. "I'm going to have another child."

A glow brightened Free's face. He pushed his chair from the table and hurried to Clara's side. In a quick motion, he lifted her to her feet and wrapped his arms around her shoulders. "That's wonderful, Clara." He hugged her tightly, "I couldn't be happier."

Clara pushed away slightly and stared into his eyes. "We will make it through this, Free. Somehow, we always do."

Free pulled her close and whispered in her ear, "I best get this work done for the army, because once I'm finished, I'm coming home, and I'm not leaving you again."

Chapter Twenty-two

Elk Creek, Indian Territory, July 1874

Maman-ti glowered as Kicking Bird departed Elk Creek with a long trailing of Kiowa people. At the sun dance's conclusion, Kicking Bird had persuaded many of the bands to forgo any further hostilities with the military and return to the reservation at Fort Sill.

Lone Wolf stood next to Maman-ti, Big Bow, and White Horse. He watched the great line of Kiowa trudge solemnly east. "What does the Owl Prophet see for my nation?" he asked, somberly.

Maman-ti's voice carried a measure of sadness, "They seem to have lost their way. They follow Kicking Bird in the hope they can live in peace with the *Tehā-nego*. But the Great Spirit abandons people who lose their path. The owl puppet tells me they will forever be known as the People who eat horses."

Lone Wolf wrinkled his forehead and kept a fixed gaze on the departing mass. "And for our kind, Owl Prophet? What does your owl medicine say?"

Maman-ti gazed at the assembled fifty warriors mounted behind them. "The owl puppet tells me fifty of the greatest Kiowa warriors stand with us. Fifty that fight like one thousand. My dreams show me seven hills near the Salt Creek. It is there that we will lure the *Tehà-nego* into a trap and share a great victory!"

The Salt Creek Prairie was a rough and rocky strip of land. Thickets of mesquite, post oaks, and black jacks dotted a rolling terrain of small hills and wagon sized boulders. The Kiowa had run their ponies hard on the journey into Texas riding two hundred miles in less than two full days.

Maman-ti and Lone Wolf led the war party into a steep ravine with running water where the warriors could slake their thirst and rest in the shade, out of the oppressive July heat.

While the warriors relaxed, Maman-ti rode out of the ravine and surveyed the open prairie. This was a spiritual land. The *ta-'ka-i* called it Lost Valley, but to him, the land held strong medicine. He planned well in his decision to bring Lone Wolf and the fifty warriors to this place. For it was here that he planned the raid on the Warren wagon train. And it was here that he and the twenty-five killed Britt Johnson. The Salt Creek Prairie had always given scalps to the Kiowa and tomorrow would be no different.

Maman-ti pulled the Spencer rifle from his scabbard and chambered a cartridge. He held the gun at eye level and focused the sight on an imaginary target. The rifle was well balanced and felt good in his hands. *You have done well for the Kiowa, Tafoya*, he thought. The gun could fire seven cartridges before reloading and would kill many *Tehà-nego* and *ta-'ka-i*.

"This is a good place for the Kiowa, Owl Prophet." Lone Wolf rode alongside the Kiowa medicine man and stared across the desolate prairie.

"The Great Spirit will confer a great victory to-morrow. I see a fresh scalp hanging from Lone Wolf's shield, and many enemy horses will perish."

Lone Wolf uttered a vicious growl, "It will be a good day to be a warrior."

Maman-ti forced a weak smile. "Yes, it will be a good day for the Kiowa."

Lone Wolf studied the medicine man's face. The Owl Prophet's eyes scrunched in great thought and lines furrowed his forehead. "I have known you for many winters, Maman-ti. What is it that troubles you so?"

Maman-ti breathed deeply, his focus remained on the tall grass waving in the breeze. "We will have our victory tomorrow, Lone Wolf. This I know."

Lone Wolf laughed slightly, "Then what causes you so much thought? It is as we hoped!"

Maman-ti turned to his warrior friend, "But after tomorrow has drifted away, the *ta-'ka-i* will return with more of their kind."

"It has always been that way, Maman-ti. We have always fought greater numbers of our ene-mies. It is what makes us strong as a people."

"But with the soldiers will come the *Teñã-nego*. The *ta-'ka-i* can be reasoned with after battle, but the *Teñã-nego* are a soulless people who carve up the land and kill for pleasure. These are peo-ple I fear."

"We will fight them until we are none," Lone Wolf snarled.

"Yes, we will, Lone Wolf," Maman-ti turned to-ward his old friend, "But what of our people? What will happen to them after we are none? They cannot keep their souls when they are forced onto government lands. How will the Kiowa warriors survive without the hunt? Will Lone Wolf eat the horse meat the *ta-'ka-i* throws at your tipi?"

"Drive these thoughts away, Maman-ti. The warriors trust your medicine. Do not give them doubt with your blessings tomorrow."

Maman-ti nodded, "*Àho*, Lone Wolf. My words will be as strong as the buffalo bull, and the Kiowa will see a great victory tomorrow. But remember, I am forced to see many tomorrows, and sometimes that dulls my vision of today."

The sun rolled onto the morning sky in a fiery show of yellow. Maman-ti led the war party across the upper ridge of the seven hills the owl puppet had showed him in his vision. The warriors moved through the mesquite and boulders without a flitter of grass or leaf.

Across the prairie, a gleaming of sunlight reflected from the rifles and pistols of a large party of men riding out of the dry creek bed to the south.

Maman-ti's eyes darkened at sight of the group, and he showed his teeth. "It is the *Teħà-nego* Rangers." He looked at Lone Wolf, "Good. They have found our trail." Maman-ti waved his hand and motioned for the warriors to spread out in a semi-circle around the rocks. He maneuvered the warriors so that half would be behind the hated Rangers. "Lone Wolf, you and I will go into the valley and show ourselves to the *Teħà-nego*."

Lone Wolf smiled. His decision to follow Maman-ti was not made because he believed the medicine man's claims of prophet, but instead because he knew Maman-ti to be the greatest battle planner of all the Kiowa. Each battle success made

Lone Wolf a stronger chief within the Kiowa nation and a hated foe of the *Tehä-nego*.

Maman-ti turned and spoke to two warriors, Mamadayte and Hunting Horse, "Wait until the Rangers give chase. When they reach the mid-point of the valley floor, bring half of the warriors down upon them. Leave the other half in the rocks to rain bullets onto the Rangers. Do as the Owl Prophet says, and we will have our promised victory."

Both warriors nodded their understanding. Mamadayte had ridden with Lone Wolf during the previous year when the chief's son, Tauankia, and his nephew, Guitan, were killed by the *ta-'ka-i* Fourth Cavalry. He understood the fire of revenge that dwelled in Lone Wolf's heart, and he was determined to make their raid today a success for his friend and chief. Mamadayte issued the Owl Prophet's instructions in a series of hand signals to the hidden Kiowa warriors.

Maj. John Jones, along with Capt. G. W. Stevens, and a group of twenty-seven young, shave tail Rangers of the Frontier Battalion trailed a set of unshod pony tracks. The major had pushed his men out the day before on word that Comanche were raiding in the area and had attacked a group of cowboys near Oliver Loving's ranch.

Earlier that morning, the Rangers had discovered a large set of pony and moccasin prints near a small pool of water fifteen miles to the south of Lost Valley.

"Major," Capt. Stevens called out. "I don't think we're following the same Indians who killed that cowboy out on the Loving spread."

"Why's that, Captain?"

"There are too many prints." Capt. Stevens pointed to the ground, "This here is a big group, and they don't appear to be worried about leaving sign."

Maj. Jones studied the tracks and rubbed his chin deliberately, "You might be right." He glanced cautiously at a rock monument situated on a small hill to his right. He recognized the marker as a memorial that covered the remains of the Warren wagon train dead. A small shiver tingled along his spine as he realized his battalion rode on the same trail where the seven teamsters had been massacred and defiled by the Kiowa.

"Capt. Stevens, send a couple of men ahead and see if the trail holds fresh as they approach the hills."

Capt. Stevens nodded and signaled for volunteers. Three men rode forward and moved ahead of the group. As the valley floor slowly turned to rock, the once visible trail disappeared. Looking back, one of the scouts shouted, "They've dried up, Captain!"

Maj. Jones stopped the Rangers and studied the landscape ahead with hesitation. After a brief moment, he called out, "OK men, spread out and let's locate their trail!"

Capt. Stevens watched the men disperse from their column and begin the search for sign. He glanced ahead and squinted, unsure or not if his eyes were playing tricks on him. A hundred yards ahead, two Indians decked in full war garb sat atop ponies. He shaded his eyes and muttered to Maj. Jones, "My Lord. Look there, sir."

Maj. Jones glanced over at Stevens and wrinkled

his brow. He then slowly turned to the north end of the valley and saw the horsed warriors. "Jesse!" he muttered, and then called to his men, "Look up, boys! The red devils are ahead of you, and there'll be plenty for all!"

To a man, the Ranger battalion raised their eyes from the trail and spotted the now fleeing ponies. Inexperienced in Indian fighting, the group immediately gave chase.

"Wait!" Capt. Stevens reined up his mount, recognizing the Indian ploy, "You're riding straight into a trap!"

Chapter Twenty-three

Lost Valley, Texas, July 1874

The Kiowa warriors screamed down from the hills and met the Rangers head on. The unsuspecting Rangers found themselves surrounded without cover and trapped in Maman-ti's snare.

Lone Wolf and Maman-ti turned their ponies around and charged back to the fight. Two Rangers immediately went down under a ferocious hail of gunfire. Maman-ti saw the Ranger commander regroup and begin a hurried scramble through the back of the Kiowa line, attempting to reach the cover of the dry creek.

Maman-ti signaled for the warriors to close their positions and cut off the path to the creek, but the desperate Rangers managed to push through and reach the gully. The Rangers scrambled from their horses in utter panic and jumped into the dry creek bed.

Maman-ti signaled a Kiowa retreat to the cover of the hillside boulders.

"Wait!" Lone Wolf screamed out, "We have them off their horses in the creek bed! Don't rush away now!"

Maman-ti threw a hard glance at his friend, "Don't be foolish, Lone Wolf. We have the *Tehà-nego*

Rangers where we want them. They hide under the high bank of the creek but are dismounted. And the only water hole is over a mile away. We will wait them out and take their scalps one by one."

Lone Wolf glared at the Rangers and bit hard against his lip. "OK! OK!" he snarled and then rode toward the hill.

Later, with both sides firmly entrenched, the fighting turned from the chaos of face-to-face combat to occasional back and forth sniping. The July heat settled firmly on the land and descended into the thicketed creek bed like a gruesome weight. Even at a distance, Maman-ti could hear the suffering moans from the thirsty Rangers.

He turned to Hunting Horse and said, "Have the warriors shoot all of the Ranger horses still above the creek bed."

Hunting Horse nodded and soon the methodical sound of rifle fire filled the air as the Kiowa began to kill the Ranger mounts.

Lone Wolf looked to Maman-ti. "Those are good horses for the taking. Why kill them?"

Maman-ti grinned diabolically, "Without their ponies, the Rangers will have to run for water. We will make them suffer in the heat until their mouths crack and their tongues swell. And when they finally decide they must have water, we will swoop down on them and take their scalps. For that is why we rode to Texas, old friend."

As evening shadows began to cross the valley, the sweltering heat lingered on and prolonged the suffering of the Ranger battalion. The Kiowa warriors sat in the hills and laughed at the misery of their enemies in the creek bed.

At twilight, Lone Wolf caught a glint of movement on the east side of the creek. In a blur of black and white, he spotted two mounts galloping from the water hole. The Rangers' white hats flashed through the grapevine thicket and exposed both riders. He motioned for Mamadayte to give chase, and soon twelve warriors raced to the valley floor hurrying to cut off the riders before they returned to their battalion.

The whoops and yips of the pursuing Kiowa spooked the mounted Rangers. One horse reared and refused to run, while the other Ranger made a hasty retreat to the south.

Mamadayte kicked at his pony's flank and surged past the other warriors. He raced head-on for the frightened Ranger and using his long lance, separated horse and rider. With the Ranger down, he jumped from his pony and raced to the prone figure, first to count coup. With his courage noted by the others, he drew back the lance and drove it deep into the terrified Ranger's chest.

Lone Wolf and Maman-ti arrived in quick haste and observed the dead *Tehá-nego.*

"I offer the *Tehá-nego* Ranger's scalp to Lone Wolf." Mamadayte pointed at the dead man.

Lone Wolf growled at their prize and sang loudly.

Oh, Great Father,
Thank you for this victory.
I honor my son and nephew with
the scalp of my enemy!

"Good." Maman-ti spoke, "You have done good, Mamadayte."

Lone Wolf pulled a brass hatchet-pipe from his breechcloth and shook the weapon at the sky, "Let us remember our dead from the Adobe Walls!" he shouted.

Chapter Twenty-four

Catfish Creek, Texas, August 1874

Under a torturous sun, Free and Parks rode alongside a Tonkawa scout, who called himself Johnson. For the past hour, they spurred their ponies down the banks of the Salt Fork of the Brazos en route to the camp of the Fourth Cavalry. The summons from Col. Mackenzie had come two days earlier, and both men rode with anxious thoughts about their meeting.

As they cleared a sweeping bend in the river, Johnson reined his pony west and followed a small creek for several hundred yards until an encampment rose into view. The camp was as austere and bleak as the country that surrounded it. Several fires flickered in the morning heat, but not one tent stood pitched, although at least four companies occupied the area.

Parks looked over at Free and spoke from the side of his mouth. "Mackenzie has gained the reputation of whipping the Fourth into the best unit in the army."

Free studied the camp and thought back to his war days, "Well it's severely simple; I'll give it that."

Johnson heeled his pony hard and bounded off the horse in a quick motion. He grabbed the bridles of Horse and the Comanche mustang and motioned toward four men sitting on cut oak trunks at the far end of the camp. "Kenzie," he said.

Free and Parks dismounted and walked toward to the colonel.

The slight officer stood as the men approached. "You must be Anderson and Scott," he said with typical military assertiveness. "Please, let me introduce you to Capt. Beaumont, Second Battalion, Capt. McLaughlen, First Battalion and my chief of scouts, Lt. Thompson." The colonel swept his hand toward the men.

"Captains. Lieutenant," Free and Parks responded with a quick tip of their hats and then straddled a pair of oak stumps.

Even after being in the field for several weeks, Col. Mackenzie appeared well groomed with neatly trimmed hair and moustache. "Sorry to bring the both of you so far from your homes, but the army needs your help." He extended a welcome hand toward Free.

Free noticed the colonel was missing two fingers on the outstretched hand. "War injury?" he asked.

Mackenzie pulled his hand back and looked at the two stumps. "A shell fragment hit me at Cold Harbor. I won't complain though, as many men suffered much worse."

Free nodded.

"Do you know what the Kiowa call me, Mr. Anderson?" Mackenzie returned to his seat and flicked his wrist, snapping the two damaged fingers against one another.

Free shook his head.

"Mangomhente."

Beaumont, McLaughlen and Thompson lowered their heads and remained quiet.

"It means bad hand. I think I might be the only officer with such a nickname by the hostiles," he mused. "Were you in the war, Mr. Anderson?"

"Palmito Ranch, Colonel. Both Parks and myself."

"Ahhh." Mackenzie reflected, "Col. Ford and Col. Barrett. That was a very interesting battle. It was too bad for the Union that Col. Barrett was so inexperienced."

Free smiled knowingly and pulled the leather pouch from around his neck. He removed a plug of tobacco and sliced a corner from the packed leaf. "Chaw?" he asked politely.

Mackenzie removed the cut tobacco from Free's knife and pushed the brown square deep into his jaw. "I'm sure you are both aware that Gen. Sheridan has ordered five columns to advance on the Texas Panhandle," he stated without extravagance. "The depredations by the different bands have finally hit a nerve in the highest offices of Washington."

Parks pushed his hat back and raised his eyebrows. "Begging the Colonel's pardon, but has Washington ever considered the possibility that continually breaking the 1867 treaty might be the cause of these, as you call them, depredations?"

Mackenzie smiled and then tightened his mouth, "I'm a soldier, Mr. Scott. I don't try to figure who did what to whom and when. I only follow orders. And at the present time, my orders tell me to move north to the canyons and scourge every cliff and crevice and find the exact place where the hostiles winter."

Free looked perplexed. "And when you find these camps, what then, Colonel?"

"They go to the reservation, or we kill them," MacKenzie replied with little emotion. "But I can tell you we are close to ridding the prairies of these hostiles."

"Excuse me, Colonel, but I don't think you and I are biting from the same plug of tobacco." Free reached up to his hat and scratched under the wide brim.

"I can tell you we are close, sir."

"Colonel, my parents were born free people, yet lived as slaves. I was born a slave, but live free. My son was born free and will live free . . ."

"I appreciate your commentary, Mr. Anderson, but as I stated earlier, my job is to remove the hostiles from Texas."

Free flushed and narrowed his eyes. "Even if you run all the hostiles to the reservations, Colonel, tomorrow another order will come from Washington and another hostile who looks different or believes different than you will need chasing. Ridding the prairie of these hostiles is your great hope, but for me and the people you chase, it's just another day to fight for things the good Lord gave us outright."

"I understand you share a unique relationship with many of the Kiowa and Comanche bands, Mr. Anderson, and I applaud you for that as I too respect the determination of their warriors. But, in the past few months, we have seen normal raiding parties turn into murdering attacks. The tribes have so increased their forays that we now count them daily. And so, Washington has ordered me to make them stop. And you can be sure that if needed I will hound the bands such that no rest came will ever come to them."

"Do you think you can really accomplish that, Colonel?" Parks asked. "This is a large country."

"Mr. Scott, my men have hardened themselves on this country. We have staggered through it, across it, around it, and up and down it. We have lived through drought, thunderstorms, spring snows, little sleep, and very little nourishment. We live like the very hostiles we pursue so vigorously. The men of the Fourth know the parties responsible for keeping them in such conditions. They will respond as needed in this campaign. I promise you they will be successful. I won't let anything less happen."

Free considered the colonel's words, "And so what is it you expect from us?"

"I need for the two of you to locate your friend White Horse. I need for you to go into his camp, and then I need for you to come back and detail the camp location for me."

Caught off guard, Free stared incredulously at Mackenzie. "Colonel, we got mixed up in the fighting at Adobe Walls, and the Kiowa know this. We no longer hold favor with White Horse. If we ride into their camp, they'll kill the both of us."

Col. Mackenzie rose and spread a tight smile, "That's the least of your worries, Mr. Anderson." He removed a folded piece of paper from his jacket, "For if you refuse this order from Gen. Sheridan, I have the authority to place both of you under arrest for consorting with an enemy of the United States during wartime."

Chapter Twenty-five

Catfish Creek, Texas, September 1874

Free bristled, "You're arresting us?" he asked, incensed.

"If I need do so, Mr. Anderson. The choice is yours to make."

"That's some choice, Colonel. Ride into a certain death or rot in an army stockade."

Col. Mackenzie checked the sun's position in the morning sky. "Mr. Anderson, my companies will began pushing north within the hour. You have until that time to inform me of your decision."

Free watched the colonel turn and walk away with a military stiffness. "That is one arrogant, little man." Free spit tobacco juice at the colonel's tracks.

"We've got some thinking to do, Free, and we best be quick about it." Parks shielded his eyes and glanced at the sun.

Free fell back on the oak stump and rubbed his face with both hands. "What now? What choices do we have?"

Parks grabbed his wide brimmed hat, dusted it against his pant leg and took a seat next to Free. "You know this is exactly why I never took a wife."

"What?" Free looked up, stunned.

"Don't get me wrong. I envy you having a woman like Clara and a son like William Parks to share your life, but I always worried about falling into a situation like we seem to have landed in today. No cowboy should be made to ride a pony like the one the colonel has saddled for us."

"Are you telling me you didn't ever marry because of Mackenzie?"

"Men like him, Free. I figure we're here because there are more people involved than just you and me. And because of that we're not left holding much of a poker hand. And Mackenzie knows that. Now, if it were you and me alone, we'd just scatter out of here and take our chances. But we can't do that; you've got Clara and William Parks to think about. And that is what Mackenzie is betting on."

Free lowered his head and stared angrily into the dust at his feet. "I reckon that's so, Parks. And it does burn my neck that Mackenzie has us saddled so."

"I have a hunch though," Parks slapped his hat back on his head. "A hunch that Mackenzie may not have it all figured out like he thinks."

Free stood and whirled away from Parks, seething in building anger. "Well unless your hunch can solve our problem today, it appears we're fixing to cut sign for the army," he muttered.

Parks stood and placed a hand on his friend's back, "We'll ride north to the canyons for the colonel all right, but while we're out searching, we best be thinking about how we want this thing to end."

"I don't follow," Free searched Park's face for an answer.

"Five columns of soldiers are pressing toward the Palo Duro. And those canyons won't only be holding warriors, Free. They'll also be full of women and children." Parks walked briskly over to Horse and swung the reins over the mustang's neck, "And I'll be hanged before I lead the army on top of them."

Chapter Twenty-six

Antelope Hills, Indian Territory,
September 1874

Maman-ti sat at the head of a council of Kiowa chiefs assembled near a long sweeping bend of the Canadian River. He balanced his palms against his knees and rocked in a steady rhythm, gently inhaling the rising fume from the council fire. As the gray cloud darted and swirled in the morning air, he fanned two cedar branches and pulled the wispy smoke toward his body. He patted the smoke under his arms, along his neck and around his chest, bathing in its cleansing power. When he completed the ritual, he used one of the cedar branches to etch two parallel lines in the soft earth.

Gray Horse, a Cheyenne brave, stood behind the Owl Prophet with his arms folded across a breastplate of eagle bones.

"Our Cheyenne brothers send word they have caught the *ta-'ka-i* Miles at the Prairie Dog Fork." Maman-ti pointed to the first line in the dirt, "Once again, the *ta-'ka-i* have made a great mistake in their planning as Miles has exhausted his food supply." Maman-ti pointed to the second line, "And now he sends wagons back to Camp Supply for much needed provisions."

Lone Wolf smiled at the news. He felt certain Maman-ti had already come up with a plan that would guarantee a successful raid on the *ta-'ka-i*. He glanced around the council and was pleased to see most of the war faction chiefs present. Maman-ti's visions and their favorable outcomes had managed to unite the Kiowa war chiefs. Something no other chief had accomplished.

"So does the Owl Prophet propose we attack Miles while his men suffer from lack of food?" Big Bow sneered, "or do we simply wait for them to starve?"

Maman-ti ignored his detractor and jumped to his feet. "No, the owl puppet says if we ride here," he pushed the cedar branch into the earth at the far eastern point of the second line, "we will be able to lay siege to his lightly protected supply wagons."

Maman-ti lay in shade beneath a formation of sandstone and gazed into the harsh glare of the morning sun. On the horizon, the dust of the army supply wagons spiraled skyward and pinpointed their positions. He glanced at Lone Wolf and motioned for the field glasses taken from the killed *Tehà-nego* Ranger at the Lost Valley fight. He placed the glasses against his eyes and focused on the slow-moving column of men. "They form two lines with their wagons."

"How many?" Lone Wolf asked.

"Thirty-six wagons and twenty mounted *ta-'ka-i*. They ride two men in each wagon."

"And what does the owl puppet tell you?"

Maman-ti handed the glasses back to Lone Wolf and looked at the readied warriors, "Are our women and children in a safe position?"

Lone Wolf nodded his assurance.

Maman-ti raised his eyebrow, "Where are they?"

"They are moving south and west to the far bank of the Washita."

Maman-ti shook his index finger at Lone Wolf. "Make sure you send enough warriors to guard them on their journey. Never forget what *ta-'ka-i* like Custer have done to other peoples. They will swoop down on our families and take their lives if they are exposed."

"You worry too much, old friend. The women and children are well protected."

"A man can never be careless and worry too little with a foe as the *ta-'ka-i*, Lone Wolf. We must be prepared to move the women and children to the winter camps soon."

"You win this battle, Owl Prophet, and let me worry about the women and children."

Maman-ti returned his gaze to the wagons intently watching their movement and held his hand into the wind. "We will set up a line of warriors on the next crest," he spoke trancelike, "When the time comes that they try to circle, shoot their mules and horses first. The owl puppet tells me this is key to our victory."

Lone Wolf uttered a laugh through a tight mouth and let his eyes narrow in the understanding of the Owl Prophet's plan.

"While your first line keeps the soldiers occupied, take one hundred warriors and move west and south to the Washita. That is where they will be most vulnerable to our attack."

Lone Wolf surveyed Maman-ti's proposed plan and showed his teeth. "You have planned well, my friend." He threw his gaze to the assembled warriors and motioned for several rifles to take up positions at the front of the knoll.

Maman-ti continued to study the supply wagons. He was determined to make them pay dearly for every inch of ground they covered from this point forward. "Lone Wolf," he called out, "let the first line fire their Spencer rifles."

Capt. Wyllys Lyman sighted the Indians by accident. A reflection of sunlight flashed into his eyes and alerted him to the presence of hostiles. He knew the importance of the provision-laden wagons to Col. Miles and understood the Indians knew this as well. He heeled his horse and waited for his second in command, Lt. West, to ride up close.

"Lieutenant, there are hostiles ahead. I don't know how many, but I need for you to move a small column of men ahead to act as skirmishers."

Lt. West nodded and began calling out soldiers' names. When he had the men chosen, he pushed ahead of the supply wagons.

Capt. Lyman turned his pony and rode in between the line of wagons shouting out instructions, "Each of you, listen closely; we have sighted Indians ahead. Stay no more than twenty yards from the wagon in front of you. If we are attacked, I want these wagons corralled as quickly as possible."

As Lt. West reached a position seventy-five yards in front of the wagons, the plunking of carbines began to pop small circles of dust from the ground.

"It's begun, men!" Capt. Lyman called to the wagons. "Head south toward the Washita!"

* * *

Maman-ti and White Horse pressed the *ta-'ka-i* skirmish lines, probing for a weakness.

"The soldiers are brave," White Horse said with respect. "They do not turn and flee at superior numbers. Theirs will be good scalps to claim."

Maman-ti focused on the small line of skirmishers and counted the soldiers. "These are experienced fighters. They are only thirteen in number, and yet they dig in like the armadillo and resist our charges."

"Maybe we should overpower them with many braves," White Horse offered, eager to fight.

Maman-ti dismissed the warrior chief with a wave of his hand. "Why kill any of your warriors with a foolhardy charge? Wait a little longer, White Horse. When Lone Wolf has circled behind the supply train, then we will charge the skirmishers."

In the early afternoon, rifle fire erupted from the Washita, and the supply wagons desperately maneuvered to circle. "Lone Wolf has set his trap!" Maman-ti broke into a wide smile.

In the ensuing chaos, the teamsters' mules began to fall victims to a hail of bullets from Lone Wolf's rear attack. The rifle fire and the braying of livestock filled the prairie with a frightening symphony, and the smell of death percolated through the air.

"They cannot make their circle." White Horse grinned at Maman-ti, "Lone Wolf will be able to overrun their position. Let's join in the battle!" He jumped on the captured spirit pony and with a series of yips raced for the fighting.

Chapter Twenty-seven

*Near the Washita River, Texas,
September 1874*

Lone Wolf and White Horse stood on a high knoll overlooking the supply train. Hastily dug breastworks offered minor cover for the now entrenched *ta-'ka-i.*

"Look," Lone Wolf pointed to the wagons. "They use their provisions and supplies as cover."

White Horse turned and looked for Maman-ti. "Where is the Owl Prophet?" he asked anxiously.

"He is in the trees, there." Lone Wolf motioned to a stand of scrub oak nearby. "He uses his medicine to speak with the spirit world. We must wait until he returns from the village of the dead for our instructions."

White Horse nodded and strained to see Owl Prophet in the scrub. "Do you believe in his magic, Lone Wolf?"

"It does not matter what I believe," Lone Wolf nodded his head toward the supply train, "only what they believe." A group of warriors circled the wagons and in daring fashion, charged the breastworks, screaming insults and shaking their fists at the unbelieving soldiers.

* * *

In the late afternoon of the third day of the battle, Maman-ti emerged from his makeshift medicine lodge. "What is the count?" he asked wearily.

The warriors all wheeled at his voice but remained mute.

"The count!" Maman-ti snarled, "How many dead?"

Lone Wolf stood and looked into the hollow eyes of the medicine man. "We have two dead *ta-'ka-i*, Owl Prophet. And over thirty mules and horses litter the sand."

The Owl Prophet stretched his arms outward and shook them rapidly. He looked at Lone Wolf and walked toward his old friend, "Then we have stayed here long enough."

"But we have them surrounded and waiting for death, Owl Prophet. We must not quit now," Lone Wolf protested.

"They sit near the river, and their wagons are loaded with food. The owl puppet tells me we cannot starve them before replacement soldiers move to this spot. We must leave now with our victory intact."

Big Bow emerged from below the ridge, ripe for an argument and shouted loudly, "No! No more running away from the soldiers, Owl Prophet! They wait for their deaths, and you want us to flee like women?"

Maman-ti looked over the assembled warriors. A gathering whisper drifted among the group. "Is this what you wish? To stay and fight? Those charges you make on the *ta-'ka-i* without injury, do you think Big Bow gives you the medicine to hold the soldier's fingers from their triggers? If you stay and fight, you will see many of your friends die in the sand of the Washita. Mangomhente pushes from the south and Price from the west!" Maman-ti made an imaginary circle with his forefinger. "Look east. Davidson rides from Fort Sill and Miles fights the Comanche just a short distance away. If we stay, they will kill your women! If we stay, they will kill your children!"

Big Bow made a slashing motion down his chest. "If what you say is true, Owl Prophet, then we must ride to Elk Creek. For it is there our women and children will have safety!"

"No!" Maman-ti cautioned sternly, "We must take the women and children into the canyon. We must join with our Comanche and Cheyenne brothers. The owl puppet warns that only there will our people be safe!"

Big Bow tossed an arm skyward and jumped to his pony. "I hope Owl Prophet is right. Big Bow will meet you in the canyon, but first I am going west and join up with the Comanche, who are not afraid to fight the *ta-'ka-i* soldiers!"

Maman-ti stood with arms folded as a small contingent of warriors followed Big Bow away from the knoll.

Lone Wolf whispered to Maman-ti, "It appears you have an enemy in Big Bow."

Maman-ti continued to watch the departing chief and then replied, "That is Big Bow's way; he goes to release his anger on the soldiers and that is good. Don't worry; he will join us later, the owl puppet has already told me this."

"Then we should begin to move to the canyon." Lone Wolf swung up on his horse and looked once more at the supply train.

Maman-ti studied the large assembly of Kiowa

and looked south. "It is dangerous to travel in such a large group. Divide into smaller bands, and meet us after three moons at the narrow canyon below the twisting path of the Comanchero, Tafoya. As you travel, fight any soldiers you come across; keep them occupied until Lone Wolf and I can escort the women and children safely into the canyon."

Chapter
Twenty-eight

South of the Washita River, Texas,
September 1874

Under the heat of a mid-morning sun, Amos Chapman arched his back in an attempt to shift his drenched buckskin shirt to a more comfortable position. He heeled his horse behind a small stand of scrub and placed his ear into the wind. The hairs on his neck and arms tingled with a warning that he normally heeded. The half-breed scout searched the northern sky and observed the building storm clouds.

"We best find some cover, Amos. These mustangs of yours hold up well, but even they can't outrun a Comanche pony after traveling all night."

Amos turned slightly in the saddle and nodded to his old friend, Billy Dixon. Dixon had quit hunting buffalo after the fight at Adobe Walls and joined the army as a civilian scout. "I know, Billy, but look at that blackened prairie. I can't say which, lightning or Indians, but it's burned to a crisp, and a tick would be lucky to find a hiding spot out there this morning." Amos wondered how Col. Miles and the men of the Sixth Cavalry were faring. He figured the colonel had made a big mistake by chasing after the Cheyenne and leaving his supply lines staggered so far from his main fighting columns. Now he was charged with the improbable task of finding the provision wagons returning from Camp Supply.

Billy stared across the scorched earth and pulled the bandana from his neck. "You think Capt. Lyman is north of the river?" he asked, as he ran the linen cloth across his brow.

"That's my best guess." Amos pulled the army issued canteen to his lips and took a long drink of the warm water. "That scattered rifle fire we heard last night had to be coming from the captain and the supply train."

"Shouldn't we ride toward them, Scout Chapman?"

Amos looked back at one of the privates who Col. Miles had sent along as couriers.

"Pvt. Smith!" Zachariah Woodhall, a seasoned sergeant, hollered gruffly, "Keep your pie hole closed!"

Amos rolled his neck back and forth trying to shake the uneasiness surrounding him and replaced the canteen around his saddle horn. "It's OK, sergeant. I reckon this early morning heat has made us all a might edgy."

"I was only saying that Col. Miles sent us out to find Capt. Lyman, and if the supply train is just north of us shouldn't we . . ."

"Private!" Sgt. Woodhall interrupted, "Shut your mouth!"

Amos rubbed his temple and glanced once more at the standing hair on his arms. *Well, we can't sit here all day.* He exhaled a deep breath and even knowing better, gigged his pony and led the five-man detail into the vast openness of the prairie.

* * *

"Keep your eyes alert and your heads on a swivel," Amos turned and whispered to the detail. When he twisted back face front, he found himself staring at a large party of Kiowa heading lazily down a small knoll that lay to the north.

"Blazes!" The experienced scout cursed and reined his pony to a stop. "This is a day I wasn't expecting so soon!" Amos dismounted calmly and, with a quick flip of his wrist, flung the beaded cover from his Winchester.

Billy Dixon followed Amos' lead and rolled from his pony, rifle in hand, and methodically chambered a cartridge. "I don't know if bad luck is following you or me, Amos."

Sgt. Woodhall shot a fast glance at the approaching horde, and looking back to Amos, gasped as both civilian scouts stood, dismounted, "We're buzzard bait sitting here, Amos. I say we make a run for cover."

"We've run these horses all night, Sergeant. We'll make our stand here. Now!" Amos shouldered his Winchester.

The three privates looked to Sgt. Woodhall for orders.

"Everyone off their mounts!" Amos screamed at the enlisted men. "Pvt. Smith, take the reins of the horses and hold them with your dear life, boy. The rest of you get your rifles ready, and use your cartridges wisely or we'll be overrun in minutes."

The Kiowa terror seemed to be on top of them instantly. The report from a single gun shot blared and Pvt. Smith clutched his chest. The private wheezed once and then fell lifeless to the ground releasing the reins of the mustangs. With the first death recorded, the prairie erupted into a barrage of screaming and gunfire.

The steady and horrific screams of the Indian raiders sent shivers down Amos' back. "Grab those horses!" His shouts, dulled by the ever-increasing numbers of Kiowa arriving at the scene, went unheeded.

The mustangs, caught in the chaos of repeated gunfire and the war cry of the Indians, scattered carrying with them the detail's canteens, food, and blankets.

Amos watched the panic-struck mustang's bolt from the battle. "Jesse!" he hollered, angrily. Fully exposed to the raiding mongrels, he gritted his teeth and braced for the coming onslaught.

Chapter Twenty-nine

South of the Washita River, Texas,
September 1874

White Horse and several hundred warriors rode from the wagon train at the insistence of the Owl Prophet and headed for Sweetwater Creek. White Horse planned to let the warriors bathe and relax there before they broke into smaller bands. But as the band crossed a small butte, he could not believe the gift that appeared on the open prairie. He blinked quickly to clear his vision. When he opened his eyes again, the six *ta-'ka-i* still stood in front of him, dismounted and prepared to fight. He turned to Hunting Horse and exposed his teeth in an animal-like snarl declaring, "The Owl Prophet truly holds great power, for look what he delivers to us."

As the first line of Kiowa riders sighted the six soldiers, a mad scramble began as each warrior made a ferocious dash for the tightly bunched soldiers.

Each subsequent line followed, kicking their ponies and racing with terrifying screams and whoops. White Horse pushed his pony forward and surged ahead of Hunting Horse. "Watch now, Hunting Horse, and observe the straightness of my aim," he called back as he held the Spencer to his shoulder. Thirty yards from the *ta-'ka-i*, he took aim at the soldier holding the six ponies and fired a well placed shot at the man's chest. "AAAAii-iheee!" he shouted, "the Great Spirit holds with us today!"

Hunting Horse, his pony's reins between his teeth, raised his rifle and fired at the white Cheyenne, Chapman. He watched the army scout crumple to the ground and then rode by close enough to push on the wounded man's back with the barrel of his gun. "Heyyyyy, Amos!" he laughed. "I got you now, squaw man!"

By the time the entire band of warriors completed one pass through the soldier's formation, every *ta-'ka-i* lay wounded on the open prairie.

White Horse wheeled his horse back to the east after shooting the soldier, and laughing, called out to his brothers, "We have these intruders where we want them; let's see how bravely they die!"

Amos grimaced as a burning sensation ripped across his knee and dropped him to the ground. The pain was instantaneous, and yellow streaks flashed in his eyes. It felt like someone had taken a hot blacksmith iron to his lower leg. "I'm hit!" he called out. He rolled on his side and held his leg in both hands. Then remembering where he was, he grabbed the Winchester and chambered a cartridge. He watched in horror as the Kiowa ponies split around him and sprinted fifty yards east of the detail's position.

"Billy!" he called, "are you still above snakes?"

"Just grazed."

"And the others?" Amos asked, his mouth pulled taut in pain.

"I reckon Pvt. Smith to be killed and the other three all hit as well!"

Amos fell back and watched as some of the Kiowa warriors raced for the stampeded horses. The Indians appeared to be having great sport with the chase. "*Awww!*" he muttered loudly, "ain't this gonna be nice!"

"What are they doing, Amos?" Billy called out. "Do you see any cover?"

"There's a stand of mesquite a couple of hundred yards to the west." Billy frantically searched in all directions.

"Too far."

"Well, it ain't much, but there's an old buffalo wallow a fair run to our right."

"I guess that'll have to make do," Amos called back, "Make a run for it one at a time. The rest of us will protect the man running. These Kiowa aim to play a game with us."

"A game?" Rising, a terrible fear swirled around Billy's insides. He rushed forward in a crouched position under a volley of rifle fire and arrows that plunked to earth around him.

"They know we're in a hopeless situation, so they are going to make us use up our ammunition and then come in and kill us slow like." Amos took aim for a warrior fifty yards off to his left.

"Hey Amos!" the Kiowa called from a distance with laughter in their voices, "here we come again!"

Amos fired, knocking one of the horses from under his rider. "Come a little closer, boys! I've got a few more cartridges to share with you!"

Chapter Thirty

Billy dove into the small depression shoulder first and rolled up so he faced the Kiowa horde with his rifle readied. "Com'on sergeant, no time to be lazy, show us your legs!" he called for Woodhall to join him in the wallow.

The sergeant tried to ignore the pain from the bullet lodged below his ribs and pushed himself from the blackened earth. He planted the stock of his rifle against the crisp grass and wrapping both hands around the barrel, hobbled for the protection of the wallow under a hail of arrows and gunfire. After a lifetime of running, he crumpled into the foot-deep depression and dropped beside Dixon. Breathing with great labor, he looked over the depression and fixed an anxious stare on the Indians.

"Wish a larger buffala would have rubbed here, Billy."

"Best start digging with your hands or knife, Sergeant. We need to raise a breastwork around us and quick. I'll cover the others as they make their way over."

The sergeant nodded and pulled a long-bladed knife from his boot. Within seconds, he slashed at the loose sand and began piling it on the lip of the wallow.

"Amos," Billy shouted to his friend, "can you

make it to me? There's no telling when that bunch will ride down on us again!"

"My knee is busted up pretty bad, Billy! There's no way I can make it on my own! Get the others in!" Amos hollered in a pain-ridden voice.

Billy slapped the ground above him and cursed, "Damnation!" He focused on Pvt. Rath who lay near the body of Pvt. Smith. "Rath!" he screamed. "Can you get to your feet, soldier?"

"I'm carrying a fair-sized cartridge in my hip, sir!" The private yelled, "I think I best rest here awhile!"

"What about Pvt. Smith?"

"I reckon him to be deceased!"

Billy rolled onto his back and stared at the sky, "Stay close to the ground, Rath," he called out. "We'll get you out of there soon." He twisted to his left and watched in amazement as Pvt. Harrington slithered across the prairie as fast as any sidewinder traveled.

The private reached the wallow in quick haste and flashed a wide grin as he dropped into the depression. "I didn't figure to wait on your invite, Mr. Dixon," he beamed.

"Glad you made it, Private; now help the sergeant with the breastwork." Billy glanced back at the Kiowa. "I think our friends out there are ready to make a run at us again."

By late afternoon, building clouds rose in the northern sky and signaled the possibility of an approaching storm. Billy ventured across the prairie several times and finally managed to help both Amos and Pvt. Harrington into the wallow. The men had repelled one attack after another from the Kiowa, but the civilian scout felt certain the Indians were wisely making them expend their precious ammunition with each probing charge.

Billy noticed that each wounded man was slumped against their fortification, and their breathing labored. The sand basin turned a darkish brown, discolored with the blood that oozed from each man.

"Sit up tall, gents." Billy offered, "If those savages recognize our condition, they'll try to overwhelm us all at once."

Amos looked up wearily and licked his dried lips, "I never thought I'd die in a buffalo wallow, Billy."

Billy looked at his shot-up friend and laughed hysterically, "Me, I never thought I'd be buried in one, Amos."

Amos managed to let a smile widened across his mouth and pushed his back straight against the wall of the depression. "I guess the time for feeling self pity is over. I don't aim to let those Kiowa take my scalp today."

Billy slapped his thigh at the resurgence in Amos's voice, "That's the spirit! Let's take a few more ponies from under those boys!"

"It will be very few, Billy," Amos replied. "I'm down to three cartridges. How about you?"

"Pretty near the same." Billy looked out to where the dead private lay. "One of us needs to get Pvt. Smith's rifle and ammo."

White Horse was atop his pony several hundred yards from the wallow when the rain stormed rushed over the prairie. The early blue norther unleashed a fury of lightning and bitter cold rain that caused the Kiowa chief to wrap himself in a blanket and calculate with angry eyes if Lone Wolf and Maman-ti had been given enough time to cross the Washita with the women and children.

He stared at the five soldiers sitting tall in the wallow and exhaled in exasperation. The prairie in front of him ran like a river, and the September rain continued to drop in blankets of gray. White Horse pulled his blanket tighter around his shoulders and considered one more charge on the soldiers. *The ta-'ka-i must be weak from loss of blood.* He urged his pony forward and glanced over the animal's shoulder at the flooding ground. The water swirled a foot up on the horse's leg. The rising water would slow their mustang's speed and make them easy targets for the soldier's guns.

Near sundown, a blowing chill spread across the prairie and caused Indian and white alike to shiver in the frosty twilight. Angry for not finishing the six quickly, White Horse signaled for the warriors to disperse. In the ghostly evening and using incredible quickness, the Kiowa vanished from the prairie battlefield undetected.

Chapter Thirty-one

Quitaque Valley, Texas, September 1874

Free rode along the sandy bluffs of the North Pease River through the Quitaque Valley. Small streams and springs dotted the landscape, and the recent drought-breaking rains had transformed the entire area into a giant marsh. He and Parks maintained a day's ride ahead of the Fourth Cavalry and hoped they could cut sign of the Kiowa or Comanche before Mackenzie's Tonkawa scouts.

Across the valley, the Red River demonstrated its awesome power as cliffs and craggy rock formations of red, brown and white thrust skyward. The canyons, cut by the massive forces of raging floodwaters over many eons, offered a terrifying decision for any military commander who contemplated battle on the canyon floor.

Free stared at the formidable geography and studied the rugged slopes of sandstone spread before them. "That's where I would go."

Parks looked over at Free. "What's that?" he asked.

"That's where I would hide in if the army were chasing me."

Eight hours later, the men rode upon the limestone cap above Mustang Canyon.

"Whhheeewww!" Parks whistled, "That's some drop."

Free studied the nearly vertical sides of the canyon wall. "It must be five hundred feet straight down."

"Most men would break their necks before descending five feet." Parks jumped off Horse and picked up a handful of pebbles. "It would be easier walking on a cliff of marbles." He tossed the handful of stone back into the canyon.

"But a perfect place for Indians," Free shrugged.

Parks remounted, clicked his tongue, and shook the reins gently, "All right, Horse. Let's find us an Indian trail." He urged the pony forward along the rock bluff.

Free dismounted and wrapped the mustang's reins around his hand. With careful steps, he walked along the outcropping, searching the rugged slopes of juniper and cedar for any kind of trail leading down to the floor of the canyon.

After a mile of tedious searching, an eagle screeched overhead and circled gracefully before descending toward the opposite cliff wall. Free took his eyes off the path to admire the great bird when he lurched forward unexpectedly and found himself falling toward the hard rock surface. Instinctively, his hands flew out to break his fall, but the tightly wrapped rein pulled against his right hand and rolled him to the left. The Comanche mustang balked at the pressure and tried to back away. With his movement restricted, Free hurtled into the cap rock and banged the tip of his shoulder on the jagged limestone. "Owwwhh!" he screamed in pain.

Parks turned in the saddle and saw Free lying on

the ground. "Free!" he called out and quickly scanned the cliffs around them, "What happened?"

Free rubbed his shoulder and made a pained face, "I caught my heel in the limestone," he winced.

And then a soft moan drifted from below the canyon rim.

Free froze and lifted slightly. His pain an afterthought, he pushed his left ear toward the ledge.

"What was that?" Parks reached for his Colt.

"Shhhhh." Free pointed over the rim. He looked at Parks and held his index finger to his lips.

"Uummmhhhhh." The distressed groan sounded again.

Free inched forward and gazed over the cap rock. From his stomach, a small path now became visible under the first branches of the junipers and the cascaded layers of rock. "Parks," he turned in stunned realization, "I think I found our trail."

Chapter Thirty-two

Mustang Canyon, Texas, September 1874

Free unwound the reins from around his hand and unholstered his Colt. "Help me over this ledge."

He stared at the steep descent before him.

"Uuuummmhhhhh." The groaning cut through the junipers' thick green vegetation.

"Whataya figure?" Parks rose in his saddle and gazed over horse's shoulder into the great canyon below.

"I can't say for sure." Free gripped Park's right hand and with great care slid over the canyon rim, kicking an avalanche of small pebbles downward on his descent. Four feet down, his boot touched a small foothold, and he released Park's hand. He studied the uneven rock face that surrounded him and dropped to his seat. The jagged cliff wall dropped abruptly beneath him to the game trail below. He surveyed his surroundings and realized the only way to the reach the trail was to travel across fifteen feet of steep incline.

"Here goes nothing," he muttered and pulled his boots in one quick motion toward his body. The action sent him sliding forward, and he quickly built momentum down the slope. Falling fast, he threw his left hand behind him and tried to brake his rapid freefall toward the narrow trail. Pebbles and broken pieces of juniper branches raked under his hand and caused his palm to burn. He pulled his hand from the ground and continued his uncontrollable slide directly into the trunk of a large juniper. With eyes wide and a racing heart, he kept his Colt drawn and ready to fire at any hint of trouble.

Afloat on a sea of loose rock and dirt, Free grabbed for the trunk of the twisted evergreen and encircled the tree with both arms. He ducked his head slightly and peered under the wind-bent limbs to a small trail that crisscrossed the cliff and appeared to lead to the canyon floor. He released his grip on the tree's trunk and slid the next few feet necessary to reach the path. He came to rest in a heap and rubbed his bloody left hand against his pant's leg. "Whhooooo!" he exhaled loudly.

As he dusted his clothing, the groaning reached a clear pitch and indicated the voice's obvious distress.

"Ohhhhhhhmmm." The utterance seemed small and frightened.

From above, Parks hollered, "Free! Are you OK?"

Free turned his ear down the trail and listened intently, hoping to hear the groan once more.

"Ooooouuuuhhhh." A long moan resounded from further down the trail.

Free searched frantically below him and then shouted to the cap rock, "Parks! Toss me a rope! I think there's a hurt child down here!"

A length of rope slid past the low-lying juniper branches and straight toward Free. Three loops secured a large rock that worked as an anchor to pull the rope past the vegetation.

"I've got it!" Free hollered toward the rim.

"The other end is tied to my saddle." Parks called down, "Just tug when you want me to pull you up."

Free loosened the rock weight and looped two turns of rope around his midsection. "Give me plenty of slack," he called to Parks and then gathered his feet. He studied the task ahead and, with great care, started down the narrow trail. The path was wide enough for one man and ran from north to south zigzagging along the cliff every hundred feet.

Free pressed one hand against the cliff face for balance and carefully began to traverse the incline's switchbacks. The gravel path fell away with each step and carried him down the winding path. Fifty yards down the trail, he spotted a small patch of mountain thistle. Hidden behind the thorny bush, a young Comanche boy thrashed about the ground with a pained look on his face. The boy, dressed in loincloth and moccasins, rolled about in a panic and rubbed at his upper body. Bright red welts dotted his chest.

Free approached with apprehension and knelt beside the suffering boy. "*Haits,*" he uttered the Comanche word for friend.

"Oooowwwhhhhhhh." The boy continued to groan in pain . He tried to rise and unable to do so, kicked out in desperation at Free.

Free grabbed the boy's flailing legs and held them firmly against the ground. "*Unha hakai nuusuka?*" he asked in regards to the boy's condition.

"*Wobi pinna unu!*" The boy screamed out and pointed to his welts.

"*Haa!*" Free called out in excited understanding and snatched a long bladed knife from his boot.

The boy recoiled in fear at the knife and rolled to his stomach. He kicked at Free and tried to gain his feet in a desperate attempt to flee.

Free kept a firm grip on the boy's legs and flipped him to his back. With a great sense of urgency, he scrambled up the frightened youth's legs and straddled the boy's midsection. Steady and careful, he began to run the flat side of his knife against each growing welt. With each pass of the blade, the knife unloosed a number of venom-pumping stingers.

The boy quieted as Free extracted a dozen or more bee glands. "*Ura,*" he offered his thanks, and exhausted, closed his eyes and lay still.

After several minutes of work, Free took a careful survey of the boy's chest and face. Not able to find a stinger, he flipped the boy to his stomach and inspected his back. "You're clean," he uttered with a sigh of relief. Worn-out, he slid off the boy and took a deep gulp of air.

The Comanche boy looked at Free and smiled.

Free dragged a shirtsleeve across his brow and swallowed dryly, wishing he had a canteen. He glanced back at the young Comanche and furrowed his brow in confusion. The boy's eyes suddenly rolled back toward the sky and remained fixed. With a sudden fear, Free dropped to both knees and looked at the boy's wide-eyed stare. The youth clutched at his chest and his breathing quickened. The speed of the boy's distress panicked Free, and without an afterthought, he scooped the boy into his arms and tugged at the rope wrapped around his stomach.

"Parks!" he screamed, "Pull us up! Pull us up!"

The lasso tightened immediately and jerked

him forward. Free leaned back in an effort to keep a taut pull against the rope and in an instant raced up the ledge and toward the cap rock with the unconscious boy pushed deep into his chest.

Chapter Thirty-three

Mustang Canyon, Texas, September 1874

Parks hoisted the Comanche boy to the cap rock and laid him on the limestone. He glanced at the red welts and tightened his jaw. "What's he gotten into?"

Free pulled himself hand over hand along Park's rope and appeared from below the canyon ledge. As he rolled onto the cap rock, he nodded at the boy, "Bees. He must have gotten into a mess of them; and by the welts, it appears he made them plenty mad. I reckon the cliff wall didn't offer him anywhere to run once they started stinging."

Parks looked at Free and placed his palm against the boy's forehead. "Well, we best get him cooled down before he boils. He's as hot as a pepper right now."

Free hurried for the Comanche horse and grabbed his canteen. He splashed cool water from the canteen onto his bandana and then charged back to the stricken boy. He placed the damp rag against the boy's forehead and tried to soothe the fever. "What are we going to do, Parks?" he asked with uneasiness in his voice.

Parks reached inside his shirt and removed the tobacco pouch hanging around his neck. He plucked a considerable plug from inside and pushed the chaw deep into his jaw. "We best get a tobacco poultice ready. It's the only thing that'll draw the poison out."

Free nodded and grabbed for his pouch. Within minutes, both men were applying the chewed tobacco on the boy's stings.

Quickly, large dark brown blemishes covered the boy's body. Free placed his own bedroll under the sleeping boy's head and then sat back. "I guess all we can do now is wait." He looked at the boy and stiffened his lip. "He's young, Parks."

"Don't let that youthful appearance fool you, Free." Parks leaned back against his outstretched arms and rolled his neck from side to side. "I take him to be eight or nine years old. But he can already shoot an arrow with deadly aim and kill what he shoots at."

Free shook his head. "I know, but all I see right now is my own boy lying there."

Parks smiled. "We did the best we could with what we've got, Free. That boy is Comanche and comes with a built-in toughness that we could never have. If anyone can survive that many bee stings, it'll be him."

Free nodded. "I hope so."

Parks pulled his arms back in front of him and rubbed his elbows, "We best get these horses rubbed and let them look for browse."

Free glanced once more at the sleeping boy and then rose from the limestone. "You know his camp must be close by," he offered. "Maybe we should locate it and take him there."

Parks looked out over the canyon ledge and in a tired voice replied, "Most likely they already know we're here."

Free searched the canyon around them and sighed heavily, "You figure they'll come to call?"

"Let's just hope that boy pulls through OK." Parks gestured at the boy and then pulled a woolen rag from his saddle pouch, "Otherwise you and me are going to have a time of it."

By late afternoon, the dried tobacco poultices tightened around each welt, and the boy's breathing seemed steady and regular. Free touched his hand to the boy's forehead and was relieved to find the fever had broken.

"He's going to be fine," Parks reassured Free. He recognized his friend's concern for the Comanche boy, "I told you he was a tough one."

Free smiled and nodded, "Now we've got another problem." He gazed at the rapidly setting sun.

"What's that?" Parks raised his eyebrows questioningly.

Free pointed to the west. "We're a good ride from the Fourth, and it'll be dark soon. I figure we're going to be stuck here on the cap rock tonight."

Parks tightened his jaw and stared at the sun's position over the canyon. "It appears you and I will be enjoying another dry camp, Free."

Free studied Park's face closely and grinned, "Let's see. We're a good day's ride from any help, trespassing in the Comancheria, and . . . we're holding a stolen Comanche pony and a lost Comanche boy."

"No one can ever say we do things the easy way." Parks tipped his hat back and re-saddled Horse.

"More fuss, I reckon." Free drew a deep breath, "Just more fuss."

Later, under a graying sky, Free chewed on a piece of hardtack and listened to the sounds of the night.

Parks sat nearby and took in the moonlit night of the Palo Duro. "This is some country."

"It is at that." Free spoke without looking up, "It's a big country. So large, that two groups of people could live here and never see one another."

Parks nodded his agreement. "That is a fact."

"And yet, men seem bent on trampling wherever another man wants to lay his hat."

Parks stretched his arms at shoulder level, "I guess that's one of the shortfalls of being a man." A yawn formed at his mouth, and tiredness came over his body. "We best get some shut-eye while we can."

Free looked back at the sleeping boy. "You go ahead. I'm going to spend a little time gazing at those stars." He pointed skyward, "I figure they were put there for the watching."

Parks settled back against the hard limestone of the cap rock and placed his hat over his face. "Free?"

Free turned toward his friend, "Yeah?"

"Don't be surprised if that boy is gone by morning."

"What?"

"All I'm saying is he's Comanche. When he's ready to leave, he'll just up and be gone."

"Snake people?"

"Uh huh."

* * *

In the early morning hours, a wave of weariness settled in Free's eyelids which caused him to lean back onto the hard rock bed of the cap rock. A faint smell of rain accompanied a rising north wind, causing him to tuck his arms close into his body. Across from him, Parks snored soundly, while the Comanche boy's steady breathing eased the tension of being far from home in a dangerous land. Unable to resist his body's need for rest, he closed his eyes and pictured Clara and William Parks. Thoughts of his wife and child brought a smile to his mouth and allowed the needed sleep to relax his muscles. His eyes blinked occasionally as his mind continued to struggle against the on-coming blackness, but lacked the strength to fight his body's desire.

As his mind finally surrendered, a strange and familiar voice swam lazily through his head, and a thin coolness tickled his throat. Free tried to scratch at the light sensation, but his hand was heavy and would not budge. Half asleep, he licked at his lips and pushed with all his might against the weight of his eyelids.

It was only after the slight whisper repeated itself that his eyes startled open in recognition of the voice.

"You are very brave or very foolish, buffalo man. You steal my horse and now my child." To'sa-woonit pushed the blade of a flint-tipped knife deep against the flesh of his throat.

Chapter Thirty-four

Mustang Canyon, Texas, September 1874

Free blinked rapidly and tried to adjust to the darkness and prevailing confusion. To'sa-woonit knelt on one knee directly to his right and the two stared at each other through the darkness. Suddenly, the powerful Kwahada warrior grabbed a handful of his shirt and yanked him to an upright position. To'sa-woonit flashed the knife before his eyes and snarled in animal-like fashion. "Which is it?" The Kwahada Indian's breath carried the smell of raw liver.

Free threw a quick glance around the camp. Charcoal figures moved in and out of his vision. Farther right, several shapes materialized into Kwahada warriors. Several feet away, Parks sat upright and stared unflinchingly straight ahead. Two warriors held long spears against his back.

Free looked back at To'sa-woonit and noticed the boy stood behind his father. The boy tugged at his father's shoulder and spoke rapidly.

To'sa-woonit jerked his head toward the boy and pushed him away. The two began a lengthy argument with words flying back and forth so rapid that Free could not follow the conversation. After much bickering, To'sa-woonit's face reddened and he gestured violently toward Free and Parks.

The boy drew near his father once more and

continued to plead with animated insistence, pointing to his welts and the dark sky.

After several minutes of banter, To'sa-woonit growled at Free with bared teeth, "What are you doing on Kwahada land, buffalo man?"

Free swallowed and carefully gauged his words. "We came here," he nodded toward Parks, "to warn the tribes of the Cavalry's intentions."

To'sa-woonit pulled his head back and howled in laughter. The rest of the raiding party roiled at their leader's provocation.

"We know the *taibo's* intention, buffalo man!" Tiny streams of spittle hit Free's cheek. "They wish to send us to the reservation. They wish to make us live like women." The knife blade pressed deep into the bridge of Free's nose and a small drop of blood appeared. "You cannot tell us what we already know!"

The Comanche boy jumped to his father's side and tried mightily to pull his knife hand away from Free. "*Kee*," he pleaded, "*Kee*."

To'sa-woonit stared at his son for some time and then reluctantly removed the knife. He turned his back to Free and slammed the knife onto the cap rock with a resounding clang. "You are lucky, buffalo man, that I respect my son's words." He pulled the boy to his side and ran a hand down the boy's long, dark hair.

Free sat silent, wiping the blood that now dripped off his nose and onto his lips.

To'sa-woonit signaled for the warriors to release Parks. The Kwahada warrior walked back and forth in front of Free and gently pounded one hand into the other. After several minutes of contemplation, he took a seat on the limestone and crossed his legs and then his arms. The rage that earlier simmered across his face receded and a look of grave intent took its place. "My son is called Spotted Horse. He tells me you saved his life."

Free relaxed and gathered his thoughts. "He was stung by many bees. I have my own son, To'sa-woonit and I know how it feels to see a son in pain. I could not watch any man's son suffer so."

To'sa-woonit grunted, "So now I owe you a warrior's life. That is a strong debt to a Kwahada."

"Are you truly Kwahada?"

To'sa-woonit smiled, "Are you truly a man?"

Free raised his eyebrows at the question. "Of course," he smiled.

"But once you were a boy."

Free scratched his chin and nodded his head in understanding.

"I was once *taibo*, but now I am Kwahada. These are my people." He gestured to the warriors standing behind him.

"Then believe me when I tell you many soldiers are coming. More soldiers than the Comanche, Cheyenne, and Kiowa people combined."

"We have seen these soldiers, buffalo man. We have stopped Miles just east of here. The Kiowa have halted his returning supply wagons. And your friend from the Adobe Walls, Dixon. He and his detail are at the great supply camp. Their bodies all carry the marks of copper. Even the squaw man, Chapman is there. We know of these soldiers and are not afraid."

Parks sat taller at the mention of Chapman. "Amos Chapman?" he asked.

To'sa-woonit turned and gazed at Parks. "Yes, the squaw man. He now walks on one leg."

Free shot a quick glance toward Parks and wondered briefly about Amos and Billy. He looked at the boy and decided to try once more to make To'sa-woonit understand the retribution moving for them. "Mackenzie is coming, To'sa-woonit," he said with a stark face. "He's coming for the Kwahada."

"Three-fingers?"

"Yes. He is a day's ride behind us."

To'sa-woonit rested his chin between his thumb and forefinger and appeared deep in thought. "Mackenzie is a great warrior. The People respect his courage."

"Take your families and ride from the Palo Duro. Otherwise, Mackenzie will kill many Comanche. Tell Quanah and the great chiefs that Mackenzie comes with orders to force you to the reservation or kill you all."

"The Kwahada will not be forced to do anything, buffalo man." To'sa-woonit looked up and gritted his teeth. A mixture of sadness and anger clouded his eyes.

"Tell the Kiowa and Cheyenne they must leave the Palo Duro."

"The Kiowa will not listen. Their prophet, Maman-ti, has predicted many victories and gained his people's respect. He has traveled to the dead village of dreams. His owl puppet has guaranteed their safety in the canyon."

"Then leave the women and children and have the warriors go west," Free pleaded.

To'sa-woonit's swallowed hard. "Once our women and children would be safe from our enemies. But Custer changed that on the Washita. He showed all The People that the *taibo* seek to take the fight out of us by killing our women and our children. Since that day, no Kwahada would ever leave their women and children behind."

Parks cleared his throat and looked at Free. "It's what I told you about being burdened, Free. The Kwahada are warriors. They will live or die as warriors. Nothing you or I can say will change that."

To'sa-woonit nodded and spoke with great calm, "Listen to your friend, buffalo man. I owe you a warrior's life. So take my horse and take your life. Go back to your son and stay out of these matters for after today, I no longer owe you any life." To'sa-woonit waved his finger back and forth across his chest. "That is my word."

Free realized he had done everything possible to warn the Indians. "Then I will leave the Kwahada land." He rose and placed a hand on Spotted Horse's shoulder, "I wish peace for you and your family."

To'sa-woonit narrowed his eyes and twirled his forefinger three times. The warriors seemed to melt into the blackness at the signal.

"And thanks for the mustang," Free spoke to the empty cap rock.

A disembodied voice hung in the darkness, "Don't worry, buffalo man, when I am ready, I'll return for my horse."

Chapter Thirty-five

South of Tule Creek, Texas, September 1874

Free poured a thick layer of burnt coffee into his army issued cup and took a small sip, "Whuuu." He shuddered and then remembering army etiquette remarked with a forced grin, "Now that's good coffee."

A majority of officers gathered near the fire and waited for the arrival of the Tonkawa scouts. During the past half hour, a consistent bird-like warble whistled from the north and alerted First Battalion of the scout's approach.

Under a brilliant Comanche moon, silhouettes appeared along a low butte a hundred yards from the camp. Free noticed the outlined forms and pointed to the moving figures, "That must be them."

Col. Mackenzie and Capt. McLaughlen turned toward the north at Free's announcement and viewed the approaching riders. As the outlines came closer, Col. Mackenzie stood and straightened his uniform.

Soon, the dull thud of mustang hooves carried into the camp and the Tonkawa scouts, Johnson and Job, rode into the bivouac at a slow gallop. Behind them, a third horse appeared. The horse, led by Johnson, carried a man whose hands were bound to the saddle horn.

Under the light of the full moon, Free recognized

the prisoner at once. He took a final sip of coffee as the Tonkawa dismounted and nudged Parks with his elbow. "See who that is?" he uttered from the side of his mouth.

"Uh-huh," Parks exhaled.

"Haw-lo, Kenzie," Johnson called out.

Col. Mackenzie moved from the fire and walked out to greet the scouts. "Who do you have there, Scout Johnson?" The colonel took a final drink of coffee and splashed the remainder to the ground in a wide sweeping motion. "He doesn't look to be an Indian."

"Kenzie." Johnson spread his lips to form a wide smile, "He is better than any Indian. Better than any Comanche."

Col. Mackenzie strode over to the captive and studied the man's face with careful discern. "Who is this man?"

"This is a big man, Kenzie. The Comanche call him Tafoya."

"*Ahhhh.*" Col. Mackenzie strained until a slight smile appeared, "The Comanchero, Tafoya."

Johnson nodded and pulled Tafoya from his horse. "He knows every Comanche camp from here to Fort Concho."

"So tell me, Señor Tafoya," Col. Mackenzie approached with a welcome smile and placed his good hand on the man's shirt collar, "are you here to trade with the Comanche?" He pressed the collar between his thumb and index finger as if to remove the wrinkles.

Tafoya's eyes widened at the colonel's question. "*Yo no comprendo*?" he issued in ignorance.

The colonel's smile widened and he patted

Tafoya's shirt, "I asked, Señor Tafoya, if you know where the Comanche camps are located?"

Tafoya looked around in mock confusion. "*Perdón, no comprendo.*"

Col. Mackenzie lowered his head slightly and bit on his bottom lip. "Does anyone here speak Spanish well enough to communicate with this man?" he asked in frustration.

"I can speak the language, Colonel." Parks stepped to the colonel's side and took a quick glance at the Mexican trader.

"Good. Ask him where the camps are located."

Parks faced Tafoya and showed a tight smile. "*¿Donde está el campamento de la Komantcia?*" he asked.

"*Valiente amigo.*" Tafoya looked past Parks with his response of "some friend."

Parks nodded. "*Sin elección, amigo.*"

"What are you two saying, Mr. Scott?" the colonel asked impatiently.

"Small talk first, Colonel."

"Well get to it, sir." Mackenzie ordered.

"*¿Donde está el campanmento?*"

"*Yo no se donde está.*" Tafoya shrugged feigning ignorance of the Comanche stronghold.

Parks turned to the colonel and raised his brow. "He says he doesn't know, sir. I don't think he's going to say anything else but that."

Colonel Mackenzie pursed his lips and shook his head in disdain. "Very well." He glanced back at the fire and became lost in his thoughts for a time. When he turned to face the prisoner once more, every muscle in his face was stretched tight. He pointed to an empty supply wagon and barked out a command. "Capt. McLaughlen, have some of your men tip that wagon to the ground."

McLaughlen saluted and barked out, "Sergeant, you heard what the Colonel said. Tip that wagon tongue skyward!"

Without hesitation, a group of soldiers moved around the back of the wagon and pushed down on the backboard.

Mackenzie gazed at the suspended tongue and swiveled back to Tafoya. "Now, Captain. Please escort Señor Tafoya to the wagon."

McLaughlen swept his arm toward the Comanchero and gestured with his index finger. In seconds, a group of soldiers carried a reluctant Tafoya to the wagon.

Mackenzie stared hard at his now confused prisoner. "Mr. Scott, please ask Señor Tafoya once more where the camps are located."

Parks swallowed hard in realization of what Mackenzie planned for the Comanchero. "*Amigo.*" Parks shook his index finger toward the man, "*Es muy importante! Es necesario responder a pregunta anterior!*"

Tafoya shrugged once more, "*Yo no se.*"

Col. Mackenzie folded his arms across his chest to show his impatience. "Well, Mr. Scott?"

"He says he doesn't know of the camp location, Colonel."

Mackenzie tapped his foot in restless irritation. "Captain, set me a loop of rope around that tongue." His order was made with a strange calm in his voice.

Tafoya fidgeted, uncertain if the colonel was bluffing. He uttered to no one in particular, "*Yo no se.*"

With the rope set around the wagon tongue, Mackenzie nodded at McLaughlen.

The captain understood and formed a quick noose with the free end of the rope.

"Proceed," Mackenzie ordered.

Capt. McLaughlen placed the noose around Tafoya's neck and pushed the knot tight.

"*Yo no se!*" Tafoya cried, "*Yo no se!*"

Mackenzie eyes blackened and the sound of his teeth grinding against one another issued to the now gathered First Battalion. "Go ahead, Capt. McLaughlen."

McLaughlen tossed his hand skyward and two soldiers began hoisting Tafoya toward the wagon tongue.

Free started forward but a hand swung across his chest barring his motion. He turned toward the outstretched arm and saw Parks shaking his head no.

"Wait," Parks whispered.

As Tafoya's boots cleared the ground and the noose tightened, the Comanchero's eyes and cheeks bulged into a grotesque distortion.

"OK!" Tafoya cried out in a choked voice, "OK! I'll tell you! I'll tell you! Just get me down!"

Chapter Thirty-six

Cita Creek, Texas, September 1874

The winter encampments in Mustang Canyon stretched for miles along the headwaters of the Prairie Dog Fork of the Red River. Each fall, wintering bands of Comanche, Cheyenne, and Kiowa arranged their lodges on the floor of the horseshoe shaped upper canyon. The Comanche deemed the Palo Duro as a gift from the Great Spirit. The canyon sheltered and protected The People from their enemies by five hundred feet of vertical cliff and steep trails that offered any trespasser a life threatening descent.

As was their custom, the Comanche arrived first into the canyon and camped along the junction of Cita Creek and the Prairie Dog Fork. The small clear stream offered clean water for all of the bands.

The Cheyenne settled on the main stream, and the Kiowa, who reached the Palo Duro last, made camp a mile from the Cheyenne villages.

For many winters, Mustang Canyon had also provided protection from the unpredictable and harsh Texas weather. This year, wave after wave of rainstorms moved through the Palo Duro, and turned the canyon floor into a muddied quagmire. In recent weeks, the storms brought with them bitter cold air that provided the camps with little opportunity to dry out.

In the Kiowa camp, Maman-ti woke early. A bad spirit had visited him in the night. The spirit invaded his mind and showed him a frightful vision. An endless line of *ta-'ka-i* marched down the *areca* trails and into the villages. The *ta-'ka-i* walked in front of their horses and each carried a repeating rifle on his shoulder. The canyon filled with dark smoke as they fired their weapons and a mournful chant arose from all the lodges.

Owl Prophet!
Where is your medicine this morning?
Why did the Great Spirit not pity us?
Why are the
ta-'ka-i killing us so?
Owl Prophet?

Maman-ti lay on a bed of buffalo hides and stared outside at a gray and dreary day. A slight drizzle hung in the air and water dripping from the tipi's flap formed a puddle in the doorway. The dream chant continued in his head and Maman-ti pushed both hands hard against his ears with the hope that the song would go away. After several minutes, he jumped to his feet and scrambled to the world outside.

In the soaking drizzle, Maman-ti held a hand over his eyes and trudged in gluey mud toward the Comanche village. His mind whirled with regret of bringing his people to the Palo Duro. Big Bow had arrived two days earlier in the Kiowa camps, but a rumor circulated this morning that his persistent detractor and ten Kiowa warriors prepared to leave for the staked plains with a band of Kwahada. Maman-ti knew if the rumor was true, it might show a loss of confidence in his medicine by other war chiefs.

Maman-ti entered the Comanche camp and headed for the tipi of a friend, Chief O-ha-ma-tai. O-ha-ma-tai's tipi was a magnificent structure composed of twenty-four sewn hides around four main pine lodge poles. The tipi was the largest structure within the village and on occasion, served as a meeting place for war councils.

O-ha-ma-tai sat in the open flap of his tipi and watched the intensifying drizzle outside. He was a squat man with a prominent nose and reddish skin. Flat leather cord decorated his hair and long black braids draped off his shoulders onto his chest.

"Haw-lo, Maman-ti." He scooted back into the tipi and motioned for his friend to enter. "The Great Spirit gives us much water this moon."

Maman-ti nodded tight lipped and slipped inside. "Maybe too much."

"Aw-no. The People can never have too much water." He shook his index finger from side to side. "What brings my friend here today with so much trouble drawn on his face?"

Maman-ti grinned at O-ha-ma-tai's observation.

"My face is like the rock painting, O-ha-ma-tai. A man can see the art, but sometimes it is difficult to figure out what the artist drew."

O-ha-ma-tai laughed. "Yes. That is true." He reached to his side and picked up a long leather pouch that held his pipe. He slid the hand carved pipe from its cover and packed the trough with leaf. "Come. Relax and have a bowl."

Maman-ti nodded and sat across from the Comanche chief.

O-ha-ma-tai pulled a slender burning twig from the fire pit and lit the tobacco. Facing the tipi opening, he held the pipe with outstretched arms toward the east and bowed his head. After a quiet prayer, he drew a deep lungful of smoke and blew the plume out of the tipi opening. "Thank you, Great Spirit," he prayed aloud, "for taking pity on The People." After the required offering, O-ha-ma-tai passed the pipe to Maman-ti.

Maman-ti took the pipe and bowed to O-ha-ma-tai. He took a deep puff and closed his eyes as the smoke rushed to his brain. He exhaled a great cloud of smoke and offered his thanks to O-ha-ma-tai, "*Àho.*"

"*Àho.*"

Maman-ti felt his body relax and he passed the pipe back to O-ha-ma-tai. "I need to ask, old friend; has Quanah and his band left the canyon?"

O-ha-ma-tai drew on the pipe and exhaled in a whoosh. "This very morning with Black Horse and his band. Why?"

"And does Big Bow ride with them?"

"Yes." O-ha-ma-tai shook his head, "I do not know this warrior Big Bow very much. But he was angry and sang a long chant as he left this morning. I will tell you, Maman-ti, Big Bow made some of the Comanche nervous with his chant. He sang of soldiers coming to the canyon and killing The People."

Maman-ti stared past the tipi flap, oblivious to his surroundings and O-ha-ma-tai's presence. He recalled his last encounter with Big Bow on the Washita. They argued about where the Kiowa women and children would be free from harm. Big Bow insisted Elk Creek offered the greatest protection. But Maman-ti had disagreed. He was the prophet to the Kiowa people, not Big Bow. Maman-ti could not allow any detractor to weaken his medicine by dictating where the bands would winter. Shocked by Big Bow's open challenge, Maman-ti lied and proclaimed the owl puppet had spoken to him in a dream about this very subject. He knew the warriors would heed the puppet's words.

He had broken the spirit's trust and invoked his own words as those of the owl puppet. Now, those same words rushed at him with the speed of an arrow and might destroy his people. His mouth gaped open and his eyes widened.

"What is it, Maman-ti?"

Maman-ti turned to his friend with a questioning look. "Huh?"

"What troubles you so that not even the pipe calms your feelings?"

Maman-ti closed his mouth and regained his composure. "It is nothing, old friend. But I must leave you now."

"As you say."

Maman-ti thrust his chest forward and rose from the tipi floor. "Thank you for the pipe, O-ha-ma-tai." He turned and exited with graceful confidence.

As he slogged through the mud, he reassured himself that an enemy had never breeched the canyon's shelter. He issued a false smile as he strode through the villages, but inside his stomach churned in great agitation and a throbbing pain dulled his senses.

Chapter Thirty-seven

Tule Canyon, Texas, September 1874

Under a heavy mist, Free and Parks held their horses to a fast gait and raced down a side ravine of Tule Canyon. The men had pushed their ponies hard for the past hour, running through muck and skirting fallen rock. The recent storms had left whole sections of the cliff face unstable and dangerous. They had ridden sixty miles since morning and hoped to reach the Fourth Cavalry before nightfall. The lathered ponies flung small dabs of mud into the air and the wet earth dotted both men's faces.

After the incident with Tafoya, Mackenzie demanded that all of his scouts were to stay mounted until they found a trail that would lead him to the winter camps. Over thirty Tonkawa and Seminole-Negroes scoured the Palo Duro for sign, and each hoped to be the man who handed the Comanche over to Mackenzie.

Free and Parks had remained silent about their encounter with To'sa-woonit, and prayed that the Comanche warrior would leave the canyon with his people.

As the rugged path snaked around a large deadfall of rock, the main trail of the Tule greeted the men. Without slowing, they urged the horses into the wide canyon, and rode into a quag of fresh Indian sign.

Parks pulled hard on Horse's reins and flipped the mustang's head up. Horse snorted as he slipped in the mire and came to a halt on shaky legs. Parks looked over Horse's right side and studied the muddy pool of prints. Heading to the southwest, a hundred or more unshod pony tracks littered the canyon floor. "I hope these are Kwahada tracks."

"To'sa-woonit?"

"Maybe. Or they could be Kiowa," Parks stared at the prints, "or even Cheyenne."

"Maybe To'sa-woonit listened to us and decided to leave the canyon?" Free leaned over his saddle and studied the ground.

"We can hope that's what these tracks say."

"Let's follow them, Parks, and see where they lead."

"Free, we've done all we can. We've willfully disobeyed orders by not informing Mackenzie of the Indian camp locations. And whether To'sa-woonit heeds our warning or not, the villages won't stay hidden much longer."

"But, Parks, the military has never located the winter camps before.

Even when Mackenzie chased the Kwahada here in '71, he didn't locate the main village." Free held a cupped hand upward and allowed the falling mist to accumulate in his palm. "And this weather has to favor the Indians."

"Free, you and I both know the fight is coming. We've heard gunfire all day throughout these canyons. Mackenzie is determined to locate the Indian camps this time and the '71 campaign taught him that to beat the Indians; he has to become an Indian."

"Maybe we should go to the Cheyenne and Kiowa and tell them what we told To'sa-woonit."

Parks snapped his hat from his head and dragged a sleeve across his forehead. "Dang-it, Free! Listen to yourself. You've got a wife and kid back home. We're not going to get ourselves killed by riding into the hostile villages. We've done all we can."

"So that's it? That's all? We just ride off and let the killing happen?"

Parks dragged his hat back on his head. "That's it. The Tonkawa will lead Mackenzie to the camps, Free. You can bet on that. The colonel has promised the Tonkawa all the Comanche horses and possessions they can carry once the camps are located."

"I don't figure I can just sit by while all this happens, Parks."

"You can't think like that, Free. Tafoya sealed the Indian's fate. With his directions, the Tonkawa will locate the camps. You had nothing to do with that."

Free dismounted and slammed his hat to the ground. He walked in a tight circle around the hat and flailed his arms about. "You know they're going to kill everyone in those villages, Parks!"

Parks jumped down from Horse and faced his friend. "They don't have to, Free. For as hard as Mackenzie appears, he's not a Custer or a Miles. He knows the buffalo slaughter is going to defeat the Indians. He doesn't care for massacre. He only wants to follow orders and be a good soldier."

Free stopped pacing and grabbed his hat. "And what are his orders?"

"To take the hostiles to Fort Sill."

"Then why is he pressing so hard to find the winter camps if he knows killing the buffalo will bring the Indians in?"

"Because, I figure he's set to burn every tipi in the canyon and then I 'spect he's going to capture every Indian pony."

"Whaaat?" Free began to pace again.

Parks stared upward and let the mist fill his open mouth. "I'm certain that's his intention," he swallowed and wiped his face, "No buffalo. No tipis. No ponies. No more fighting."

The sudden realization of Park's words caused Free to halt. "Mackenzie's knows the Indians can't survive the winter without horses or shelter."

Parks stepped up in the stirrups and slid onto his saddle. "Mackenzie's going to take something more valuable than their lives, Free."

"Huh?" Free wondered. "What could be more valuable than a man's life?"

"Mackenzie aims to steal their souls. An Indian who can't hunt and feed his band is a pathetic creature. Mackenzie knows this." Parks tapped his temple. "When he's finished in those villages, he'll not only have trampled the tipis, he'll have trampled the Indian spirit too."

Free seethed at Park's words. "Then I've got one more idea." He lifted the reins, gigged the Comanche pony, and galloped past Parks shouting, "We'll tell Mackenzie that we found tracks leading out of the canyon. We'll tell him we figure the bands are packing up and leaving." He whipped the reins across the pony's shoulders and raced headstrong for the Fourth Cavalry's bivouac.

Chapter Thirty-eight

Mesa Blanca, Texas, September 1874

Col. Mackenzie sat on the dead trunk of a mesquite tree and stared at Free and Parks. The men of the Fourth had set the tree near the command fire pit with the express purpose of giving the colonel a warm place to sit. The rain and mist had stopped earlier, but a chill hung in the fall air and showed itself with each soldier's breath.

Mackenzie sat upright and rigid. Deep in thought, he unconsciously flipped his wrist in a repetitive motion and caused the stumps of his blown-off fingers to pop against one another. The dull thud resounded around the camp and kept each soldier on high alert. *The Colonel was nervous and anxious.*

"You are sure, Mr. Anderson, that a hundred or more hostiles are fleeing the canyon?"

"That's what the tracks indicated, Colonel. They headed southwest out of the Palo Duro."

Mackenzie rolled his gazed to Parks. "Can you suggest why they would leave in that direction, Mr. Scott?"

"I couldn't say, sir." Parks met the colonel's gaze head-on.

Mackenzie stood and rubbed his stumps. "The Tonkawa are certain the hostiles are massing around us tonight. I think the hostiles are setting a trap for us, sirs. I learned a wonderful lesson in these same canyons some years ago."

"Yes, sir," Free encouraged the Colonel's recall.

Mackenzie moved closer to the fire and stood with his back against the warming heat. "We captured Mow-way's village, but the hostiles circled back on me and recovered not only their horses but many of my men's mounts as well." Mackenzie moved from the fire and stretched his back. "They even got my horse." He studied Free's eyes intently and then took his place back on the dead tree. "But, it won't happen again, Mr. Anderson. I'm more than prepared for their treachery this time."

Maman-ti sat in O-ha-ma-tai's tipi, surrounded by a council of chiefs. He had made a fateful decision earlier in the morning. He decided he could not risk his position as shaman and admit he had misused his power on the Washita. *It is for the good of the people*, he had told himself, and he was determined to lie again if necessary.

The Cheyenne chief, Iron Shirt, rocked gently and said, "My warriors have found many signs of Tonkawa nearby."

Maman-ti observed the honored warrior and forced a smile, "But that is a good sign Iron Shirt. The Tonks are crisscrossing the canyon and cannot locate our lodges."

The Cheyenne chief frowned. "I hate these, Tonkawa," he spoke in a soft voice, "they eat people and cannot be trusted. I wish we could kill them all."

Maman-ti nodded his agreement and looked over to O-ha-ma-tai. "The soldiers are too close.

The owl puppet tells me we must attack tonight and keep them from our lodges."

O-ha-ma-tai turned his palms upright and gently shook them up and down. "I am concerned, Maman-ti. If we show ourselves tonight," he flipped his palms over and pushed them downward, "Mackenzie will know we winter close by."

"Don't worry, old friend." Maman-ti lied, "the owl puppet gives me a great sign that the People will send Mackenzie's Fourth running like dogs with their tails tucked behind them."

"How does your puppet say this will happen, Owl Prophet?" Iron Shirt leaned forward in great anticipation.

Maman-ti gazed into Iron Shirt's eyes and then turned to his side and looked at O-ha-ma-tai. "The owl puppet tells me to attack their horses."

Free and Parks sat clustered with a group of soldiers fifty yards to the front of the horse lines. Mackenzie had placed twenty skirmish lines five yards apart and well ahead of the horses in anticipation of a night attack.

Parks pulled his tobacco pouch from inside his shirt and cut a small chaw from the rectangular plug. "Tobacco?" he motioned to the men in his detail.

"Thank you, sir." A young private took the offering, "My daddy always told me to never turn down free tabacky."

Parks grinned. "I'm sure your daddy was a smart man, soldier."

Free pushed a chaw into his jaw and took a deep breath. "I didn't think Indians attacked at night?"

"Bright as that moon is tonight, it probably seems like day to them." Parks gazed at the brilliant circle. "If they come, I reckon that the Colonel has gotten a little too close to their villages."

The private returned Park's tobacco and looked back at the horses. "Old Colonel Mackenzie seems to have these red devils figured out, sir."

Parks nodded. "You're right about that soldier. I've seen many a hobbled horse in my life, but I have never seen a horse hobbled front to front and then front to back."

"And then staked with an iron rod." Free grinned.

"I would bet a week's pay, we needn't worry about those horses stampeding tonight." Parks offered, "I just hope if the Indians do set upon us, that we don't need those ponies as mounts."

Chapter Thirty-nine

Mustang Canyon, Texas, September 1874

After meeting with the council, Maman-ti retired to his lodge and prepared to mix his war paint. As he entered his tipi, he removed a wide leather belt hanging above the flap. The belt was three feet long and painted with a line of blue owls. Spaced evenly along the belt were seven buffalo horns, each woven to the belt with horsehair, and corked with a small hide ball.

He removed an intestinal pouch from one of the horns and held the pouch at eye level. Inside was his most prized white clay from New Mexico. He squeezed a handful of the clay into his palm and began to roll the earth. When the clay formed a long cylinder, he dropped it into a pot of hot water and grease. He stirred the mixture with a willow branch until the clay bubbled into a fine mud. Using his hands as brushes, he slathered the war paint over his entire body and then stood over the fire pit. The heat from the coals penetrated his skin and warmed the paint. He held his arms away from his body and turned in a tight circle around the fire. After several passes, the fire-baked paint adhered to his body.

With the white paint ceremony complete, he removed another pouch from the set of horns.

The pouch held a concoction of berries and duck droppings. Maman-ti used the items to produce a blue color.

When the mixture of grease, blue coloring, and hot water was complete, he painted two owls beneath each breast and repeated the baking process.

With the war paint now firmly fixed to his body, he grabbed his war lance. A decorated lance would announce to war chiefs and warriors that Maman-ti had received a vision from his spirit guide. Maman-ti sat on a buffalo hide and laid the twelve-foot spear across his knees. He tied hawk feathers and long streamers of white cloth near the flint tip with woven horsehair.

To complete the ritual, he sat cross-legged at the fire pit, closed his eyes, and began a low chant.

> Owl puppet, hear my prayer.
> Show me my enemies, killers of Kiowa
> women and children.
> Owl puppet, show me the way
> to defeat this foe.
> Owl puppet, hear my prayer.

After some time, Maman-ti rose and marched from his tipi. His face was rigid and taut. He mounted his horse and began to ride through the lodges chanting to his people in a loud voice.

> Where are the warriors?
> Where are the Kiowa?
> It is the day to go to war.
> It is the day to defeat Mangomhente.

He circled family bands of tipis in the camp and continued his chant.

It is the day for great honor.
Where are the warriors?
Where are the Kiowa?
Who wants to ride down to the Fourth?
Who wants to count many coup?

The rain, long since quit, had left in its wake the crisp cool air of fall. Upon hearing the chants, many Kiowa left the warmth of their lodge fires to watch the Owl Prophet.

Lone Wolf was the first outside. Wrapped in a buffalo robe, he smiled at the painted body of Maman-ti, and rushed to his friend's side. "Has the owl puppet given you a vision?"

Maman-ti looked down at his friend, "Yes. The owl puppet tells me to go to Mangomhente's camp this very night."

Lone Wolf raised his arms and shouted to the gathered crowd, "What are you waiting for? Go prepare your paint. Go prepare your lances. For today, the Owl Prophet has had a great vision!"

A loud cheer reverberated in the camp and young Kiowa warriors, eager to ride with the Owl Prophet, raced to their tipis to prepare for the war party.

"What is your plan, Maman-ti? How will we attack Mangomhente?" Lone Wolf asked, excited by the prospect of battle.

Maman-ti let a rush of confidence flow through his body. He looked at Lone Wolf with his mouth pulled tight, and snarled, "We scatter his horses and capture them for our own. Let Mangomhente see how it is to be in the canyon during winter without a horse."

Lone Wolf lifted his head and issued a long howl. "It is a good plan, Maman-ti. A plan that will bring many Cheyenne and Comanche to fight with the Kiowa tonight."

Beneath a Mexican moon, two hundred warriors rode in complete silence for the camp of the Fourth Cavalry. The two hundred were dressed in full war regalia and presented a terrifying visage to any enemy.

Five hundred yards from the Fourth's camp, Maman-ti stopped the war party and issued a final reminder. "Scatter the horses first. Do not get caught up with counting coup or killing soldiers until the horses are running."

The warriors all nodded their understanding.

Maman-ti looked at the camp and moved his pony slightly forward of the war party. *It is Maman-ti who is the great planner, not the Owl Prophet. It is Maman-ti who will be honored after tonight,* he thought in quiet. And then, Maman-ti nudged his pony forward and the attack began.

The warriors streamed across the prairie and raced for the cavalry camp. Protected by the Owl Prophet, they no longer worried about noise. The warriors, filled with energy, shouted in loud whoops and hoots, announcing their presence to the Fourth Cavalry.

Parks slapped Free's elbow. "Here they come!"

Free jerked his eyes ahead and looked north.

On the horizon, hundreds of Indian ponies charged their way. "Be alert, men!" he called to the skirmishers. "The Indians are riding for us."

Volleys of rifle fire began to pop in the clear air and the commands from the skirmish lines were heard from a thousand yards away. In a matter of minutes, the Indian charge rushed through the skirmish lines and headed for the camp's corral.

"Well, I'll be," Parks uttered. "The Colonel was right. They aim to stampede the horses."

Colonel Mackenzie was up at the first whoop. He sprinted for the live horse corral and shouted at the soldiers sleeping there, "Come alive! They're upon us!"

The men jumped to their feet and grabbed their rifles. Under the Colonel's orders, all of the Fourth slept fully dressed this night and were prepared to meet the charging horde. The soldiers moved in and out among the nervous horses, and using the steeds as cover, took careful aim at their Indian foes.

"You outsmarted them for sure, Colonel," a soldier hollered at Mackenzie.

"Hold the line." Mackenzie called out his orders in a cool and collected fashion.

The soldiers inside the corral positioned and repositioned their firing angles inside the herd.

"Keep a horse between you and the hostiles," Mackenzie ordered.

The war whoops and the chaotic gunfire spooked the staked and hobbled horses. The cavalry mounts pawed at the ground and tossed their heads from side to side trying to break free.

"Easy." The soldiers whispered in vain attempts to calm the horses. But, the animals, confused by the activity, continued to tug against their ropes in a desperate attempt to get loose.

After the initial charge, the Indians began to circle and then retreated to a small ravine where they spent the next four hours firing with little enthusiasm at the men of the Fourth Cavalry.

As dawn entered the Palo Duro, a clear day opened under a sky of intense blue. Col. Mackenzie had walked among all of his lines during the night and encouraged the men to be ready. He knew his soldiers were struggling to stay alert after enduring a long march and no sleep over the past twenty-four hours. Still, he felt a momentous victory was close. The hostiles had fired infrequently during the night and now sat in a ravine only three hundred yards away.

He stared at the sky and allowed a wide grin to come over his face. Satisfied as to the day, he replaced the smile with a hard look and strode with serious intent among the men of E Company.

"Capt. Beaumont!" Mackenzie barked. "Why are you resting in your sacks when there are hostiles on the horizon firing their weapons at our camp?"

Beaumont jumped up and called his men to their feet. "Saddle up!" he shouted, "Capt. Boehm get your men to action!"

Mackenzie followed the men of E Company onto the prairie. He walked along side their horses and called encouragement to each soldier.

As he passed the first skirmish line, he called out, "Mr. Anderson and Mr. Scott. Go with these boys and see if you can locate a trail for me."

Free and Parks stood saddled and packed. Both

had anticipated an early march from the colonel this morning.

Free nodded and stepped into his stirrups. "Begging the colonel's pardon," he tipped his hat as a courteousy, "but I can't ride through two hundred warriors to look for sign."

The colonel stared across the prairie. "Don't worry, sir. These boy's will have those hostiles on the run shortly." Mackenzie swung his head toward Free, "And when they do, E Company will break off the chase and wait for the rest of the Fourth Cavalry. Once we have overhauled our rations we'll continue."

Parks looked over to the colonel. "You're purposely going to chase the hostiles and then stop to take time to re-supply?"

"That is correct, Mr. Scott," Mackenzie's voice rose in frustration.

"And, we're supposed to follow the Indians? All two hundred of them?"

Mackenzie allowed a tight smile to form near the corners of his mouth. "Well, you are scouts, Mr. Scott. And isn't that what scouts do?"

Chapter Forty

Mesa Blanca, Texas, September 1874

Parks spurred Horse with unrestrained vigor for Capt. Boehm and E Company. Free followed, whipping the reins back and forth across the Comanche pony's shoulders in an attempt to keep abreast of Parks.

E Company had covered the three hundred yards to the ravine in quick time. With Colts drawn, they began to fire upon the hostiles from fifty yards away.

Realizing the ravine was now a death trap, Maman-ti issued a series of yips, signaling the war party to retrieve their staked ponies. The warriors broke from their cover and sprinted up the far side of the gully toward their horse lines.

Parks and Free caught up with E Company above the ravine and accompanied the cavalry into the wash; they rode in a thick blanket of smoke and dust. The clang of hooves on rock thundered through the ravine as the men of E Company raced up the back wall and onto the flat prairie above.

"There they ride!" Capt. Boehm shouted.

The Indians fanned across the prairie in a horse line over a mile long and raced toward the beckoning horizon. A whirlwind of dust spiraled behind each mustang and left a haze of white earth drifting head high in the morning air.

"Will you look at that?" Free called out in amazement.

Parks shot a quick glance at his friend and replied, "They tied brush to their mustang's tails before the fight."

"Somebody up there knows a thing or two about warfare." Free replied.

"Watch now." Parks motioned toward the fleeing ponies.

All of a sudden, the dust line elongated and stretched from east to west as far as the eye could see.

"They're splitting up," Parks remarked and began to ease up on the reins, "They might go two hundred different directions now."

Free reined the Comanche pony in a spray of loose rock and stared at the distant cloud.

Capt. Boehm and the men of E Company galloped by Parks and Free and continued the chase for another three miles before stopping. Boehm and his men suddenly found themselves staring out onto an empty prairie. Many of the soldiers twisted in their saddles to see if the Indians had circled back.

"What the—?" Capt. Boehm removed his hat and scratched his head.

Parks trotted Horse toward the troops and turned to Boehm. "You need to get faster horses, Captain."

"I don't see how they disappeared so quick." Boehm shook his head in disbelief.

Free made his way for the captain and Parks. "Listen to that silence. It's as if they were never here."

"What now, Captain?" Parks asked.

Boehm dipped his head, turned to his command and yelled, "E Company! About to Second Battalion!"

E Company regrouped into three lines and waited for the captain to move to the lead position.

"What about you two?" Boehm asked.

"I reckon we're going scouting. I'd rather face ten Comanche than the colonel this morning," Parks grinned.

"You're a smart man, Mr. Scott." The captain laughed and rode to the front of his men. He lifted his right hand and motioned forward, "E Company, Ho!" he shouted, and then swiveled in his saddle, "Good luck to you both."

By midday, Free and Parks stood on the overlook above Mustang Canyon.

"I figure the Indian camps are further down river," Parks said. He held Horse's reins and walked the mustang along the cliff.

"Past where we found Spotted Horse?" Free asked.

"I think so." Parks studied the cliff wall with a careful eye.

"We must be a good eight hours from the Fourth." Free scanned the juniper underbrush growing along the cliff and said, "The Indians were smart to attack so far from their camps."

"I just hope it was enough to keep Mackenzie off the trail," Parks replied.

"Once he gets something into his mind, I don't believe there is a safe distance from the colonel," Free said. He edged his way along the cliff pushing juniper limbs aside as he went. "How far do you think we've walked from where we found the boy?" he asked.

"Maybe two miles. Why?" Parks asked as he made his way around the overgrown trees.

"Over here," Free called out.

Parks fought his way through the juniper and found himself standing next to Free. Five hundred feet down the cliff face, hundreds of sheep-like creatures milled about on the canyon floor. Parks stared at the animals puzzled. "Are those sheep?" he asked.

Free pointed to the specks, "Those? Those are ponies," he said, "And those," he swept his arm to the left, "are tipis."

Parks moved ahead of Free and leaned out over the ledge. He looked as far down the canyon as possible and let out a low whistle. "There must be four hundred lodges in that valley."

Free nodded and followed the ragged ledge for a hundred more yards. He cut through another stand of juniper that opened onto a large patch of limestone. Unlike the surrounding rock, the limestone's surface here was smooth. Free moved to the edge of the cap rock and surveyed the wall. Below, a narrow trail, two feet wide, zigzagged down the canyon.

"Parks."

Parks pushed through the juniper and tossed a questioning look at Free.

Free nodded his head, "This is it."

Parks walked to the ledge and spied the path. "I'll be."

"What now?" Free asked.

Parks rubbed his chin and thought for a second. "I think we should ride away from here. We need to head back to the Tule and find those tracks heading to the southwest."

Free stepped into his stirrups and turned the Comanche pony south. "I reckon that's a good idea," he said.

A group of warriors waited with great impatience outside of Maman-ti's tipi. Lone Wolf stood guard at the tipi entrance and faced the angry mob with crossed arms.

"Where is he?" Mow-way screamed.

"He is speaking with his spirit guide." Lone Wolf spoke in a calm voice, "He will speak with to all of us when he has received another vision."

"We have twenty dead because of the Owl Prophet!" Mow-way threw his hands up in disgust, "Twenty, Lone Wolf!"

Lone Wolf felt the tipi flap slap against the back of his legs. He raised the flap's corner and peered inside. He nodded his head several times and then turned to Mow-way.

"The Owl Prophet will speak to us now."

Inside the tipi, the warrior chiefs gathered around Maman-ti's fire pit and sat on twelve buffalo hides spread over the ground.

"My spirit guide has come to me in a dream." Maman-ti spoke with calm in his voice. "The spirit tells me that we were betrayed by one of our own last night."

A great murmur circled the tipi. A betrayal by a warrior was unheard of.

Mow-way jumped to his feet and looked about the warriors gathered. "Who?" he waved his hand around the group, "Who would betray their own, Owl Prophet?"

Lone Wolf looked with great confusion at his friend and gazed into his eyes.

Maman-ti returned Lone Wolf's stare with eyes as black as night. "Look around, Mow-way and see which of us is not present."

Lone Wolf drew a deep breath and raised his fist in anger. "Who, Owl Prophet? Name this warrior!"

Maman-ti shook his head no. "I cannot. The spirit does not allow so. The spirit will take care of this traitor. We remain safe from the ta-'ka-i. Our villages remain unseen by Mangomhente."

"Is it Big Bow?" Lone Wolf shouted out.

"I can speak no more on this, Lone Wolf. The spirit commands me. I can only say look about you. Who is not with us?"

Parks and Free led their ponies away from the prints left by the Kwahada warriors two days earlier.

"Take it slow, Free." Parks cautioned, "I want the Tonkawa scouts to pick up our tracks in this canyon today."

"You really think Mackenzie will believe these two-day old tracks are for real?"

"If we can make him believe that the war party last night was a ruse, that the Indians wanted to occupy the Fourth's attention, so their women and children could make it to safety . . . then yes . . . our plan will work."

After spending a good hour planting tracks both in and out of the canyon, the men rode up the trailhead for the cap rock. "Now, we just need to catch up with the Fourth." Parks turned in the saddle and surveyed the country behind them.

"What are you looking for?" Free asked.

"I just want to make sure no one trailed us." He searched east and then gazed south.

A mile or so away, a thin dust cloud dispersed in the air. Parks yanked the field glasses from his saddle horn and lifted them to his eyes. "Jesse!" he hollered out in frustration.

Free leaned in close. "What is it, Parks?" he asked.

Parks slumped in the saddle and let the glasses drop from his eyes. "It's those two Tonkawa, Johnson and Job." He pushed the glasses toward Free, "I reckon they've been on our trail since we left E Company."

Chapter Forty-one

Tule Canyon, Texas, September 1874

Job poked at the dried earth in Tule Canyon and shook his head to show his mistrust. "I don't believe this, Kenzie."

Col. Mackenzie sat at the front of two columns of soldiers. He took a hard gaze at Parks and Free and then back to his Tonkawa scout. "Job, You're a scout. Do those tracks show the movement of the tribes or are they merely a band of renegades running buffalo or who knows what?"

Free gigged his pony forward. "Colonel?"

Mackenzie turned and flicked his hand upward. "What is it Mr. Anderson?"

"My read on these tracks is this bunch left out of here two days ago and in a hurry. It's like they were spooked, and I know the other bands would not stay knowing this."

Mackenzie studied the tracks in great deliberation and then said, "It's a matter of trust, Mr. Anderson. Whom should I trust? You, Tafoya, or the Tonkawa?"

Parks smirked at the colonel's comments and eased Horse forward. "Superstition, Colonel," he offered.

Mackenzie wheeled in his saddle. "What's that?" he asked.

"The Indians are all superstitious, sir. If one

band left, as Free said, then they would all leave out of here."

Mackenzie straightened in the saddle and sat silent for a time. The soldiers all recognized the familiar snapping of his stumps against one another. "Very well, Mr. Scott." He bore his gaze into Parks, "Let's proceed to the head of this canyon."

Hunting Horse and Mamadayte peered down into the canyon and watched as the *taibo* soldiers moved southwest. Hunting Horse smiled as the darkness prepared to cover the Palo Duro. "Maman-ti was right once more, Mamadayte. See, Mangomhente leaves us."

Mamadayte exhaled in relief and jumped to his pony's back. "The council will want to know of this, Hunting Horse. Let's go back and share the good news."

As nightfall blanketed the Fourth, Mackenzie halted the columns and shouted to the forward scouts, "Johnson! Job! Come back here."

Parks and Free, who rode behind the Tonkawa, stopped and glanced at one another.

"What's up?" Parks whispered.

The Tonkawa split off from the forward scouts and rode back to the colonel.

"I can't say," Parks shrugged.

The colonel conferred with the Tonkawa and then called to Parks and Free, "Mr. Scott. Mr. Anderson. Please come back this way. There's been a change of plans."

Free and Parks turned their horses and rode back to Mackenzie.

"What's going on, Colonel?" Free asked.

"I think we've followed this trail as far as we need to."

Parks leaned forward in his saddle and studied Mackenzie's face. "But this trail leads right out of the canyon, Sir."

"That's the problem, Mr. Scott. This trail will not lead us to any hostiles. I think the camps are behind us."

"And you arrived at that conclusion, Colonel after marching for hours down the Tule?" Free asked.

"No, Mr. Anderson. I arrived, as you say, at that conclusion before we ever began this march."

"Well then, I am confused, Colonel," Free said as he leaned back in his saddle, "Why go so far out of the way if you know where the camps are located?"

Mackenzie smiled. "You know that answer, Mr. Anderson. It was you who insisted we ride this way."

Free frowned. "What are you saying, Colonel?"

Mackenzie's pushed the smile away and gritted his teeth. "I'm saying we've been watched for the past few hours from above."

Free threw his gaze to the darkened cliffs.

"They're gone now, Mr. Anderson." Mackenzie relaxed his jaw and leaned in close to Free. "They've ridden back to the camps to give the all clear. Mangomhente is leaving the canyon they will say. But, Mangomhente is not leaving." Mackenzie looked back to Beaumont and McLaughen. "Captains! Move your companies right. We're marching back into Mustang Canyon."

Chapter Forty-two

Mustang Canyon, Texas, September 1874

As dawn broke over the Palo Duro, the Tonkawa scout, Johnson, peered over the smooth worn limestone ledge above Mustang Canyon. "Many Indians, Kenzie," the scout called out.

Col. Mackenzie turned to Beaumont and grinned, "Captain, you will follow the scouts down with two companies of Second Battalion and I'll lead the other two."

Beaumont rose, turned high in his saddle, and sang out, "Com-pa-knees! Disss-mount! A and E come with me. H and L follow the colonel."

Mackenzie turned to McLaughlen and waved his hand across the cap rock. "Captain, hold First Battalion on top for cover."

McLaughlen nodded. "Yes sir."

"And Captain," Mackenzie motioned at Free and Parks. "Keep an eye out for these men. Don't let them wander too far from First Battalion."

"Yes sir," McLaughlen snapped.

Mackenzie dismounted and walked to the cliff ledge. The new day had arrived clear and bright. He turned to his chief of scouts and with a great calm said, "Mr. Thompson, take your men down and open the fight."

Maman-ti gazed from his tipi at the bright, cool day outside. He rose and stretched his arms, grateful he had managed to retain his status as shaman. In the distance, a whoop echoed around the canyon followed by a lone gunshot. *Crazy Comanche*, Maman-ti thought. After weeks of fighting and running, today promised to be a day of calm.

He stepped outside and rolled his shoulders from side to side. The cool night air had stiffened his muscles and made his neck ache.

After several minutes of stretching, he heard his name being shouted from the edge of the village. Maman-ti stopped and listened as a pony came racing into view.

"Owl Prophet!" The horse's rider called out from a distance, "Mangomhente is coming!"

Maman-ti's heart raced and lightness settled in his chest as he made out the rider. "What is it, Hunting Horse?" he cried out.

Hunting Horse raced straight for Maman-ti, jerking his reins at the last moment and causing his pony to stumble. "It's Mangomhente!" Hunting Horse screamed. "He's riding through the Comanche lodges with many soldiers!"

Maman-ti stared beyond Hunting Horse and watched as the Kiowa people began to flee their tipis. He swallowed hard and slapped at Hunting Horse's pony. "Get the warriors and run to the cliffs. From there we can fire down on Mangomhente!"

Hunting Horse nodded and pulled his horse around.

"Go!" Maman-ti yelled as he raced for his rifle.

Free and Parks looked down at the chaos unfolding on the canyon floor. The Tonkawa and First Battalion had reached the camps in quick time. On the floor, they remounted and moved in four sweeping lines through the villages.

"My God!" Free said, horrified.

Comanche warriors scrambled for the cliffs while the women and children attempted to carry armloads of possessions with them.

From his left, Free heard Capt. McLaughlen bark out, "First Battalion! Move out!"

In a organized scramble, First Battalion began its single file descent to the canyon floor.

"What do we do?" Free asked Parks.

Parks looked back to the unfolding battle and then searched the rim. "I don't know. Let's move down the ledge and see if any of the women and children try to gain the top on this side."

Free nodded and picked his way through the line of men waiting to enter the trail.

Both men rode a mile down the rim and watched as Mackenzie moved from lodge to lodge. "Look." Free pointed to the forward line of First Battalion. "Where are they going?"

A group of soldiers hurried away from the main skirmish line and raced straight down the canyon.

Parks grabbed his field glasses and trained them on the departing soldiers. "That's Beaumont. He's riding to beat the devil that's for sure."

Both men continued to trail the fight along the canyon ridge. They rode in step with the Fourth as the running battle moved southeast out of the camps.

Two miles past the Kiowa village, a dark cloud

raced head on for the skirmish lines of the Fourth. Parks raised the glasses again and swallowed hard. "Look at this." He shoved the glasses toward Free.

Free peered down into the canyon and inhaled deeply. "Sweet spirit!" he exclaimed, "There must be a thousand horses running in that herd!"

Chapter Forty-three

Mustang Canyon, Texas, September 1874

By late afternoon, the fighting had stopped and the Indians had disappeared into the Palo Duro. Free and Parks rode through the sacked Comanche village amidst a blur of activity.

Black smoke rose from a pyre of burning lodge poles. Grease from the Indian fire pits had soaked into the supports over many years of use and now the animal fat climbed to the canyon rim in a sickening fume. The soldiers from H Company worked like a line of ants, depositing pole after pole onto the burning heap.

The fleeing Comanche had left in their wake a trail of flour, blankets, pottery, and buffalo robes.

The Tonkawa and Seminole-Negro scouts rummaged through the flattened tipis looking for bows, lances, and knives. An occasional cheer went up as a scout found a decorated shield.

Parks and Free observed Col. Mackenzie standing on Cita Creek sponging his neck with a dampened scarf. Both men dismounted and walked over to the victorious commander.

"I guess you're to be congratulated, Colonel." Free said.

Mackenzie wrung out his scarf and straightened his back. "I think things turned out well for the Fourth today, Mr. Anderson."

Parks looked back at the looting Tonkawa. "And the Tonkawa or so it appears." He turned and smiled at the colonel.

"Don't be too hard on those men, Mr. Scott. The Comanche normally hunt them as prey. Give them their day."

Free nodded and said, "The horses you recovered, Colonel. Where did A Company take them?"

"I ordered Capt. Beaumont to take them back to Tule Canyon, Mr. Anderson. Why?"

"I need to ask a favor, Colonel. I know you won't understand, but please hear me out."

"Go ahead," Mackenzie replied.

"I think my horse is in that herd, sir. It was taken by the Kiowa at Adobe Walls some months ago and I would ask the colonel's permission to search the herd for my horse."

Mackenzie's jaw tightened. "I'm afraid that won't be possible, Mr. Anderson."

"May I ask why, Colonel?"

"Because, Mr. Anderson, I gave Capt. Beaumont permission to cut out three hundred of the best animals and distribute them to his men."

Free swallowed hard. "What about the others, sir? Maybe Spirit's in with that group. If you could just give me a little time to look."

"I'm sorry, Mr. Anderson," Mackenzie said. He straightened his shirt and walked toward the middle of the Comanche village.

"You're sorry?" Free followed in disbelief of the colonel's sincerity.

"I'm sorry," Mackenzie answered without looking back, "For I also ordered Capt. Beaumont to shoot the remaining horses."

Chapter Forty-four

Anderson Homestead, Texas, November 1874

Free sat at the kitchen table and took a drink of coffee. "So, you're sure about this?" He poked at a piece of paper lying on the table.

"I think it's time for me to do something different, Free."

"Well long distance racing is definitely something different," Free chuckled. "But I know you'll fare well."

"We both need some time to do some of the things we've dreamed about," Parks said.

Clara turned from the stove with the coffee pot in her hand. "Who wants more?" she asked.

Free held out his cup and grinned, "I do."

Clara poured his cup full and then motioned the pot to Parks.

"No more, Clara, thank you."

From outside Dog began barking, and William Parks ran to the back door. He peered through the screen with his hands cupped over his eyes. "Daddy?" he asked, "Where are you?"

Free laughed. "William Parks, I'm right here. What do you want?"

"I want to tell you a man took your horse."

"What?" Free jumped to his feet and raced for the door.

William Parks jumped back as Free stepped

outside. "Over there, Daddy." He pointed to the horse pens.

Free ran to the corral with Parks and Clara on his heels. "What the—?" he looked back at Parks.

Inside the corral, Spirit stood, tied to the corner post with a horsehair rope. Free swiveled his head in all directions trying to catch a glimpse of the man William Parks spoke of. "Who brought Spirit back, son?"

"It was a man, Daddy. He said to tell you he came for his horse."

Free looked at William Parks in bewilderment and then turned to Clara.

"Don't look at me," she shrugged.

Free stepped on the lower rail of the pen and scanned the prairie once more.

"Are you thinking what I'm thinking?" Parks asked.

Free shook his head from side to side in disbelief and hopped down from the rail near Spirit. He chuckled and rubbed the mustang's nose. "Good boy," he said.

Free turned and lifted William Parks to his shoulder. He grabbed Clara's hand and looked Parks straight in the eyes. "Snake people," he said with a wide grin.

Author's Note

Only three Indian fatalities were recorded during the September 28 battle in the Palo Duro Canyon. However, Mackenzie did succeed in crushing the soul of the native people camped in the canyon that morning by destroying the lodge poles and horses. Mackenzie, in a bold, strategic move left the Indians afoot and without shelter for the upcoming winter months. By November, the starving hostile bands were forced to re-think reservation life.

Between October of 1874 and March of 1875, most of the Comanche, Cheyenne, and Kiowa had either surrendered or been captured.

- Big Bow surrendered to authorities at Fort Sill in early February of 1875.
- Maman-ti and Lone Wolf surrendered to authorities at Fort Sill in late February of 1875.
- White Horse surrendered in April of 1875.

Kicking Bird targeted Maman-ti and Lone Wolf as seditious and both received prison sentences along with five other Kiowa chiefs. It is said, the other sentenced chiefs asked Maman-ti to place a death wish on Kicking Bird for his betrayal. One week after the Kiowa chiefs were interred at Fort Marion in Florida, Kicking Bird died in Indian Territory. Maman-ti died soon after.

By May of 1875, only one major band of Comanche remained at large, the Kwahada. On June 2, 1875, Quanah Parker led the remaining four hundred Kwahada into Fort Sill and surrendered themselves and fifteen hundred ponies ending the Red River War.

After the Palo Duro Canyon battle, Ranald Mackenzie defeated the Cheyenne in the Black Hills War (1876) and subdued the Apache in Arizona (1881). In December of 1883, Mackenzie became a patient at the Bloomingdale Asylum for the Insane in New York. He died in 1889 at a cousin's house. Ulysses S. Grant called Mackenzie, "The most promising young officer in the army."

All six men at the Battle of Buffalo Wallow were awarded the Congressional Medal of Honor. Later, congress revoked the medals of Amos Chapman and Billy Dixon, as both men were civilian scouts. Billy Dixon refused to give back his medal.

The use of the "Old City" refers to what archeologists now call the "Buried City."

The author chose to use the name, Mustang Canyon, as the site of the winter camps because historical records and archeological evidence remain at odds with one another. Some historians regard Canon Blanco, Canon Cita Blanca, or Canoncita as the site of the Comanche, Cheyenne, and Kiowa camps. However, present day archeological evidence cannot pinpoint the winter camps with a definitive location. Thus, the author chose to call the canyon by a fictional name.

Ambush at Mustang Canyon

GLOSSARY

KIOWA PHRASES AND NAMES:
Aho—Thank you or Kill him
Areca—Deer
Aungaupi—Buffalo
Aungaupi chi—Buffalo man
Maman-ti—Sky Walker
Mangomhente—Bad hand/Three fingers
Pééy—Dead
Teha-nego—Texans
Ta-'ka'-i—Ears sticking out
Tséeyñ—Horse

CHEYENNE NAMES:
Minimic—Eagle Head

COMANCHE PHRASES AND NAMES:
Esa-tai—Hind end of a coyote
Haa—Yes
Haits—Friend
Kwahada—Antelope eaters
Kee—No
Numa—The People
Puha—Power
Quanah—Fragrance
Tabananaka—Sound of the sun
Taibo—List taker
To'sa-woonit—Looks white
Toyarohco—Cougar
Unha hakai nuusuka?—How are you?
Ura—Thank you
Wobi pinna unu—Honey Bee

Ambush at Mustang Canyon

GLOSSARY

SLANG:

Above snakes—Alive

Barking at a knot—Wasting time

Biscuit—Saddle horn

Bone orchard—Cemetery

Cut sign—Locate the trail

Grulla—A gray-colored mustang

SPANISH PHRASES AND WORDS:

La Cueva de Comanchero—Cave of the
  Comanchero

Es muy importante—It is very important.

Es necesario responder a pregunta anterior—It is
  necessary to respond to a previous question.

¿Donde está el campamento de la komantcia?—
  Where is the Comanche camp?

Señor—Mister

Palo Duro—Hard wood

Por favor—Please

Perdón, no comprendo—Sorry, I don't understand.

Sin elección, amigo—I have no choice, friend.

Valiente amigo—Some friend

Vaya con dios—Go with God.

Yo no comprendo—I don't understand.

Yo no se donde está—I don't know where it is.

Yo no se—I don't know.

Ambush at Mustang Canyon

DISCUSSION QUESTIONS

What is the novel's theme?

How do you think the Southern Plains Indians regarded the buffalo hide hunters?

What do you think is the cause of most wars?

What do you think was the cause of the Indian wars in Texas?

Eagle Wing, a Sioux chief, said, "We have been guilty of only one sin—we have had possessions that the white man coveted." What possession did the white man covet?

Do you think the native people were hypocritical in their statements about coveting another's possessions?

Do you think all wars are political processes?

Do you consider war to be a logical step when one culture tries to control and change another culture's societal conditioning?

In the opening quote, Secretary Delano uses words such as destruction, destroying, and coercing in regards to forcing native peoples to adopt the habits of white civilization. From the quote, how do you think the United States government regarded native people?

Ambush at Mustang Canyon

DISCUSSION QUESTIONS

Explain the process of accommodation after conflict.

Explain the process of assimilation after conflict.

Explain the quote, "Once thoroughly defeated, a man is never the same again." Do you think the native people were ever the same again?

What are the two most important aspects of societal conditioning?

Does assimilation permanently displace societal conditioning?

Do you think the United States government followed the "golden rule" in their dealings with native people?